Studying every move the trio made, Clint held still until he knew that it was absolutely necessary for him to move. He'd been hoping, for their sakes, that they would let the matter drop after a few rounds of threats and tough talk.

But that didn't seem to be the case. Those three wanted to do things the hard way. It was unfortunate, but only for them. Clint wasn't good at doing things the hard way.

He was the best.

Now that one of them was about to fire, Clint decided it was time to show them the difference between talk and deeds. His hand swept upward along the side of his holster, plucking the Colt from its resting place as his fingers slid around it, placing the pistol in the prime spot for his arm and hand to draw and fire with the least amount of fuss.

DON'T MISS THESE
ALL-ACTION WESTERN SERIES
FROM THE BERKLEY PUBLISHING GROUP

THE GUNSMITH by J. R. Roberts
Clint Adams was a legend among lawmen, outlaws, and ladies.
They called him . . . the Gunsmith.

LONGARM by Tabor Evans
The popular long-running series about Deputy U.S. Marshal
Long—his life, his loves, his fight for justice.

SLOCUM by Jake Logan
Today's longest-running action Western. John Slocum rides
a deadly trail of hot blood and cold steel.

BUSHWHACKERS by B. J. Lanagan
An action-packed series by the creators of Longarm! The
rousing adventures of the most brutal gang of cutthroats ever
assembled—Quantrill's Raiders.

DIAMONDBACK by Guy Brewer
Dex Yancey is Diamondback, a Southern gentleman turned
con man when his brother cheats him out of the family fortune. Ladies love him. Gamblers hate him. But nobody pulls
one over on Dex . . .

WILDGUN by Jack Hanson
The blazing adventures of mountain man Will Barlow—from
the creators of Longarm!

TEXAS TRACKER by Tom Calhoun
Meet J. T. Law: the most relentless—and dangerous—
manhunter in all Texas. Where sheriffs and posses fail, he's
the best man to bring in the most vicious outlaws—for a
price.

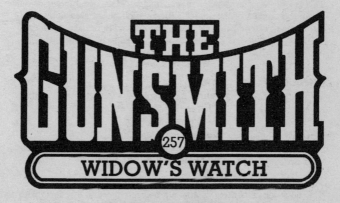

THE GUNSMITH

257

WIDOW'S WATCH

J. R. ROBERTS

JOVE BOOKS, NEW YORK

WIDOW'S WATCH

A Jove Book / published by arrangement with
the author

PRINTING HISTORY
Jove edition / May 2003

For information address: The Berkley Publishing Group,
a division of Penguin Group (USA) Inc.,
375 Hudson Street, New York, New York 10014.

ISBN: 0-515-13533-X

A JOVE BOOK®
Jove Books are published by The Berkley Publishing Group,
a division of Penguin Group (USA) Inc.,
375 Hudson Street, New York, New York 10014.
JOVE and the "J" design
are trademarks belonging to Penguin Group (USA) Inc.

PRINTED IN THE UNITED STATES OF AMERICA

10 9 8 7 6 5 4 3 2 1

ONE

The train had been thundering across the plains for what felt like an eternity. Clint Adams sat in the seat that had become his own after claiming it at the beginning of the trip several days ago. There had been no territorial disputes since then, just the forced camaraderie of a group of people all cramped together in the same box headed the same direction over a pair of metal rails.

Clint had spent a week in New York City, staying at a hotel he'd never used before. It wasn't one of the bigger or fancier hotels, but it had comfortable beds and served one of the best steaks Clint had ever tasted that far away from cattle country. Besides, he'd wanted to keep a low profile.

What he missed more than the beds and steaks, though, was the sweet redhead who worked cleaning the rooms and running errands for the hotel's owner. Her name was Killeen. As soon as Clint managed to say more than a sentence or two to her, she'd insisted that he call her Kelly. She had the dark red hair that was the color of the sky when the sun was setting and night was just about to fall. Like most redheads, her skin was creamy white and soft to the touch. As it turned out, Clint hadn't had to wait

1

too long before finding that out for himself.

In fact, Clint got to run his fingers along her skin the first night after arriving in New York City. She'd served him his meal and he'd watched the way she moved. The turn of her hips caught his attention and held it firmly. She wore loose skirts that brushed over her legs as she moved, yet hugged her hips just enough for him to savor the plump firmness of her backside. And when she turned, sending her skirts cascading around her, he could see the bounce of her generous breasts beneath the fabric of her blouse.

And like any other woman, she knew she was being watched. When she caught Clint looking at her in that way, she'd smiled and nodded without breaking the rhythm of her movements. She knew that he liked what he saw, even if she didn't know much more about him than that.

"When can you get away from here?" he'd asked, while paying the bill.

"I'm off work in a couple hours." There was no pretense on her part. Glancing past Clint toward the stairs that led up to the rooms, she added, "But I could still stay around here if I was properly persuaded."

"Come for me when you're free and we'll take it from there."

She reached out and ran the tip of her finger down his chest, ending with a friendly poke in his midsection. "I'll be there, Clint. Just make sure you're ready for me."

Before he had a chance to answer, Kelly turned on the balls of her feet and strutted back to the tables that were waiting for their plates to be taken away or their drinks to be topped off. She moved with an extra twitch in her hips, causing the material of her skirt to wrap around her bottom just enough for Clint to get a good look.

Reluctantly, he moved away from the door and headed outside for a walk to stretch his legs and some fresh air to top off the meal. He stopped by one of the closest saloons, but didn't stay too long. He wanted to be sure to get back to his room in case Kelly found some way to get off a little early.

TWO

The train whistle blew its shrill cry, which was just enough to snap Clint out of his reverie. He'd been leaning his head against the window and allowing himself to drift toward sleep. Now that the whistle had sent a little jolt through his system, he straightened up in his seat and took a look around.

At the moment, there wasn't much movement inside the car. The familiar faces of the other passengers were turned at odd angles, either in sleep or staring off into space. What little conversation there was couldn't make it to Clint's ears through the constant chugging of the engine and the rattle of the wheels.

With nothing else to do for the moment, Clint was more than happy to look back out the window. The train was racing on a long, straight stretch of track with endless prairie on either side. The grasses were burnt by the sun's rays and swayed with the winds that continually assaulted the land. Every now and then, a gust would come along that was so strong it shoved the train a bit like the hand of a gentle, curious giant. It was that very motion that put most of the passengers to sleep, and Clint found that he wasn't too far behind them.

His eyelids were heavy, but he'd gotten enough rest to keep from passing out completely. In that state of mind, his thoughts began to wander and he soon found himself with a smile on his face. It was a pale reflection of the smile he'd worn when he'd answered the knock on his door in New York later that night to find Kelly standing there in a dark violet dress.

"Sorry I couldn't get here quicker," she said as she smoothed out the front of her skirt. "I hope I didn't keep you waiting long."

"No, not at all. I played a few hands of cards at a place down the street and managed to amuse myself for a while." That was the truth. In fact, Clint had gotten into such a good came of five-card that he nearly lost track of time completely.

Kelly smiled, reminding Clint of the reason he'd torn himself away from such a potentially profitable game. "Well, now it's time to see if I can amuse you for a while."

With that, Clint stepped aside and motioned for her to come into his room. She did so, tugging the sleeves of her blouse so that they rode low and exposed her shoulders and upper arms. Looking down at her, Clint could also see the smooth, creamy surface of the top of her breasts. There was a layer of perspiration glistening on her skin, giving her a kind of sparkle that was hard to look away from.

Once she was in his room, Kelly walked over to the bed and waited until she heard the door close before facing Clint and tossing her hair over her shoulder. Her neck was a finely contoured line and a few strands of her dark red hair stuck to her flesh. "I've been thinking about this ever since the first time I saw you."

Clint moved in closer and reached out to place his hands on her arms. The contact was slight, but it was enough to send a spark through both of them. "Thinking about what?" he asked.

Kelly looked as though she couldn't wait any longer. Suddenly, she lifted her lips up to Clint's and kissed him. Pulling away for just a second, she kept her eyes locked on his and melted into Clint's arms once he wrapped them around her and pulled her tightly against him.

This time, there was a heat that passed between them as their lips touched. Her mouth opened slightly to allow her tongue to run along Clint's upper lip. When he leaned in to taste her lips as well, Clint felt her step back.

She was looking at him with her sly grin, stepping just out of his reach. "I wasn't thinking about that," she said.

Clint kept quiet and watched as she reached up with both hands to pull her blouse down to her waist. Kelly's breasts were full and round. Her nipples began to harden the moment Clint's eyes drifted toward them. She stepped back into his arms and placed her hands on his hips.

Without hesitation, Clint cupped her breasts in his hands and massaged them gently. Her skin was warm and slightly damp. When his thumbs brushed against her erect nipples, Kelly leaned back and let out a soft, satisfied moan.

Just then, Clint felt one of Kelly's legs wrapping around his thigh and moving up and down. Her hips were sliding against him as well, quickly finding the bulge at his crotch and grinding against it wantonly.

"I came here for this," she whispered, taking one of Clint's hands and guiding it down below her waist.

Clint let himself be guided, even though he'd been wanting to go exactly where she was taking him the moment he felt the heat between her legs pressed against his stiffening cock. First, she moved his hand over her side and along the material of her skirt. He didn't need to be led any further before he pulled the material up until he could reach under the fabric.

The muscles in Kelly's legs were warm and taut. Her skin was welcoming to his touch and was the only thing Clint found beneath the skirt. There were no undergarments of any kind. Just her. Clint felt her thigh and reached around to cup one of her buttocks, pulling her in even tighter against him. He kept reaching until he could slide one of his fingertips into the moist patch of hair between her legs.

Kelly let out a groan when he did that and locked her fingers behind his neck. "Oh yes," she said, while leaning her head back and grinding her hips slowly. "Just like that."

All Clint had to do was tease the delicate skin of Kelly's pussy for her to start clawing hungrily at his shoulders. It was all she could do to keep hanging on to him as he touched the insides of her thighs and then eased his fingers back to her damp vagina. The moment his fingers eased inside of her, Clint felt her entire body tense.

Suddenly, Kelly snapped her head up and looked him square in the eyes. "If you don't fuck me now, I'm going to burst."

The words were barely out of her mouth before Clint picked her up off the floor and moved her to his bed. He set her down and quickly shed his clothes while Kelly got herself ready for him. She tore at her blouse and skirt, but couldn't seem to get them off fast enough. When she saw Clint's erect penis, she hiked her skirt up to her waist and propped one foot up onto the bed.

Clint eased up to her, allowing his cock to rub along her thigh and tease her wetness as he massaged the muscles in her leg. Kelly savored the teasing and squirmed on the bed, grinding her back against the mattress while easing her hips up and down.

This time, Clint was the one who took a step back. His shirt was hanging open and several buttons were scattered on the floor. Together, they looked like two people who'd been caught up in a storm and tossed away. Clint's eyes roamed over Kelly's body. Her chest was heaving and her hands wandered over herself once she couldn't get ahold of Clint. She moved her fingers over her wet pussy and spread her legs open for him.

The soft, thick hair between Kelly's legs was the same dark red as the hair that hung down over her shoulders and face. Her fingers moved through it, seeking out the most pleasurable spots to rub gently. She never took her eyes off of him, as if daring Clint to resist her for just one second more.

It was then that Clint felt like he truly was caught up in a storm. The thought of fighting it never even crossed his mind.

THREE

As much as Clint enjoyed watching what Kelly was doing, he could only stand by for so long before he had to step forward and get his hands back on her body. He pressed his palms against her sides, running them up and down, grazing the sides of her breasts and then moving back to her hips. She squirmed slowly back and forth as he did that, closing her eyes and letting a smile widen across her face.

In a matter of seconds, Clint was on top of her. His hard cock slid between her legs and brushed against her fingers while she continued pleasuring herself. Kelly wasted no time either. She used her hand to guide him inside of her, letting out a deep moan as she felt him drive deeper and deeper into her body.

When he was all the way inside, Clint felt one of Kelly's strong legs once again wrap around him. She held him right where he was while snaking her arms around his shoulders. Clint could feel their skin where they rubbed against each other, their sweat mingling as he started pumping with increasing urgency.

Kelly's hips bucked against Clint's as they let themselves fall completely into their desires. Every time he drove into her, Kelly let out a deep-throated grunt, followed by a quick intake of breath. When his chest was pressed against her, Clint could feel the solid thumping of her heart as well as the almost desperate raking of her nails along his back.

The sprinkling of pain mixed with pleasure added an exotic spice to the sensations washing through him. Her nails weren't breaking the skin, but they were scratching just hard enough for Kelly to show him how intensely she was enjoying him. When Kelly arched her back and started groaning with her impending orgasm, Clint didn't even feel a bit of pain from her scratching. All he could feel was the wet lips between her legs clenching tightly around his slick column of flesh.

Suddenly, Kelly's eyes shot open and her leg tightened around Clint with all of her strength. At that moment, Clint pounded into her as far as he could, pushing her over the edge and sending her toppling into a powerful climax.

Kelly's body tensed and her breathing quickened. As the pleasure swept through her body, she pumped her hips even faster, working Clint's penis until he was joining her in the fit of ecstasy.

Once their bodies came to a rest, neither one of them could move. Clint lay on top of her for a moment, listening to the sound of her breathing and watching the blush spread throughout her face.

After a few seconds, Clint moved off of her and dropped onto the mattress next to her. At that moment, they both seemed to realize that they had never bothered to get out of all their clothes. Clint's shirt was open and hanging on him like it was draped hastily over the back of a chair. Her blouse and skirt were both bunched around her waist, covering her slightly but revealing just enough to make her look somehow sexier than if she was completely naked.

Kelly reflexively started to straighten her clothes, but when her fingers brushed against the bare flesh of her upper thighs, she merely traced delicate lines over her body while letting her eyes wander over Clint's. Her nipples were still hard and her eyes flashed with the same carnal hunger reflected in her naughty smile.

Clint made some adjustments of his own as well, but he simply tore the remainder of his clothes off and tossed them to the floor. By the time he'd done that, Kelly had pulled her blouse up over her head and thrown it behind her.

"No," Clint said as Kelly started tugging her skirt off her hips. "Leave that."

She raised an eyebrow at the request, but granted it nonetheless. Moving so that she was lying on the bed with her back propped up against the headboard, Kelly raised her arms and pressed her hands against the wall above her while Clint moved in to slide his own hands beneath her skirt and up along her thighs.

He took his time exploring her naked skin, savoring the feel of his fingers moving beneath her loose skirt and touching her on the most sensitive areas beneath it. Slowly making his way along her thighs and stomach, Clint eventually found his way back to the soft thatch of hair between her legs. It was warm and damp; even more so than before. When Clint lowered his mouth down to taste her, Kelly spread her legs open and ran her fingers through his hair, slowly grinding against his face as his tongue slid in and out of her.

They didn't leave the room until late the next morning. And even then, it was just to get something to eat. After all, they didn't have much time before Kelly needed to get to work.

There wasn't much time . . . but there was just enough.

FOUR

As Clint thought back to that night and the morning that had followed it, he found himself nodding off. His head slumped to one side, but he caught himself just before hitting the inside of the train's window. It was then that he realized just how tired he was. Even though the memory of his time with Kelly in New York was enough to get his heart thumping and his blood pumping, Clint still found himself fighting to keep from slipping into a dream.

He'd been on the train for days now, taking only the occasional break to stretch his legs when the train stopped for supplies or to drop off and pick up passengers at the odd station along the way. He'd been wanting to keep himself from thinking about how much farther there was to go, since that would only serve to make the trip feel longer.

Also, until now, he'd been enjoying himself by savoring the opportunity to relax. But now the train was feeling more and more cramped around him and the rattle of its wheels was getting monotonous. As if responding to what he was thinking, the engine let out a loud hiss and the brakes started groaning like a dying animal. The car shook slightly and the scenery passing by outside began to slow down.

Everyone inside the car started straightening in their seats and leaning toward the windows. At the back of the car, the connecting door opened and a scrawny man in a blue uniform stepped through.

"Next stop . . . Coyville," the conductor said in a loud monotone that had become just as familiar to Clint's ears as the chugging of the engine. "Next stop . . . Coyville."

Clint reached out to tap the conductor's elbow as he walked by. "Excuse me. How long before we reach Byrne?"

The slender man stopped and cocked his head, pondering the question for less than a second. "Coyville's next in line, Mr. Adams. Byrne is right after. We should get there just before sundown." With that, the conductor tipped his hat and continued down the aisle, chanting his mantra until he was cut off by the slamming of the door at the front of the car. "Next stop . . . Coyv—"

Turning his eyes toward the window, Clint was just in time to see the first hints of the station at Coyville, Kansas. A large hook swept by Clint's window with a newly delivered bag of mail dangling from it. Next came the station itself, where a few short lines of people waited for the locomotive to stop. There was a coal chute extending down from a silo beside the track at the far end of Clint's field of vision. The train came to a stop with the second car positioned beneath that chute to receive more fuel for the engine. By this time, Clint knew the sounds and motions to come like it was some kind of well-rehearsed dance routine.

There was the hissing of the pistons as they let off excess steam, the tweeting of the whistle, followed by the rumble of doors opening and feet shuffling on and off the car. Clint also knew he could get up and take a walk outside for a minute or two before they pulled away from the station again, but he decided against it. Being this close to his destination, he didn't want to get off the train until he could stay off of it. Anything less than that would just be a cruel tease to his tired body.

So while the train and its passengers went through their routine at the Coyville station, Clint lowered his hat over his eyes and crossed his arms over his chest. Before he knew it, his mind was drifting back to New York City on the day right before the train ride had started.

Kelly was a few hours into her work shift and Clint had taken some time to kick back at the saloon he'd found the day before. Surprisingly enough, he managed to pull together all but one of the players in that poker game he'd been forced to leave and didn't have any trouble at all in convincing them to pick up where they'd left off.

"Back for more, eh?" one of the card players said, even though he'd lost the most when he and Clint had last gambled.

The rest of the players chuckled at that and nodded to Clint by way of saying hello.

On second thought, Clint really wasn't too surprised at all that he'd found them there. The men might have been nice enough fellas and friendly card players, but they were still wearing the same clothes they'd had on the day before and their breath was almost potent enough to knock Clint on his backside when he exchanged greetings with them.

"You men aren't big on breakfast, are you?" Clint asked, only half-jokingly.

The first man snorted and held up a glass half-full of dark brown liquid. "I gots my breakfast, lunch and dinner right here!"

In general, Clint wasn't too big on whiskey, but the stench drifting out of the other men's mouths was strong enough to crawl down his throat through his nostrils and give him a bad taste on the back of his tongue. It wasn't a pleasant experience by a long shot, but there was a way to make it a little more bearable at least.

"Tell you what," Clint said while sitting down to a card table and signaling for the bartender. "First round's on me. Coffees all around."

The players took their seats and grumbled at Clint's choice, but weren't inclined to turn it down. It seemed that two of the four men were thinking that sobering up might not be a bad idea. The other half seemed physically unable to refuse a drink they didn't have to pay for—no matter what it was that filled the cup.

With the saloon's burnt coffee grinds on the other men's breath instead of its stale whiskey, the air surrounding the card table was much easier to bear. Clint played through several hands, and by lunchtime, three of the four others were starting to slump in their seats as the effects of their day-and-a-half-long binge began to seep in.

Clint excused himself and headed back to the hotel for some lunch and to check in with Kelly. First, however, he went up to his room to splash some water on his face. As he was patting a towel to his forehead, he heard a knock on his door.

"Come in," he said, turning to get a look at who was there.

His suspicions were correct and it was Kelly standing there looking in. His first reaction was to smile, but when he saw the look on her face, that smile quickly faded.

"What's wrong?" he asked.

FIVE

Her normal smirk was gone. Although her dark red hair still framed her face like the corona of a sunset, it didn't seem to have the normal glow that Clint had come to appreciate. That was due mainly to the fact that Kelly's expression was deadly serious and her eyes were tainted with just a hint of reluctant sadness.

Clint threw the towel down and went to her. All he had to do was open his arms and Kelly was there within them. She squeezed him tightly only one time and then took a step back. Although it didn't look as though she was going to cry, she seemed darkened by some kind of distant sorrow.

"What is it?" Clint asked again. "What's wrong?"

She shrugged and held up her right hand. It was wrapped tightly around a piece of paper folded twice as if it was about to be slipped into an envelope. "A message came for you," she said. "By telegraph. It just got delivered a minute ago and I thought . . . you should see it right away."

Clint's mind raced with all the things that could be written on that paper to get such a reaction from the pretty redhead. With his experiences in life, Clint was hesitant to let his own imagination run wild and opted to just read the message for himself.

The paper felt crisp and was still warm from where it had been clutched in Kelly's hand. He unfolded it and held it out so he could take it all in. The words were scribbled in a quick, practiced hand and were printed so neatly that it was better than some typeface that Clint had seen.

TO CLINT ADAMS **STOP**

I HOPE THIS MESSAGE FINDS YOU AS IT TOOK SOME DOING TO TRACK YOU DOWN **STOP** A GOOD FRIEND OF YOURS MY HUSBAND ROBERT DAWSON HAS BEEN KILLED **STOP** THE MURDERERS ARE THREATENING TO KILL ME AS WELL AND I KNEW OF NO ONE ELSE TO ASK FOR HELP BUT YOU **STOP** PLEASE COME TO MY HOME IN BYRNE KANSAS AT YOUR EARLIEST CONVENIENCE **STOP** IT IS A MOST URGENT MATTER AND I AM NOT THE ONLY ONE IN DANGER **STOP** I HOPE YOU WILL HELP US AND WISH TO SEE YOU VERY SOON **STOP**

YOURS TRULY

JENNIFER DAWSON

When Clint was done reading, he looked up and found Kelly still staring at him, her eyes filled with concern.

"I couldn't help myself from reading it when it was given to me to bring up here," she said apologetically. Moving in close enough to touch him on the arm, she added, "I'm so sorry to hear about your friend."

"Bobby was a good man and we helped each other out a bit some time ago," Clint said. "But I haven't seen him for several years now."

"But that message. It sounded like—"

"I know. Bobby was the type who . . . grew attached to folks pretty quickly." The fact of the matter was that Clint had almost forgotten about Robert Dawson completely. He'd met up with the man when he and his wife were in a spot of trouble some time ago. A killer and a few of his murderous friends had decided to pick a fight with Dawson because Robert was not a fighting sort and seemed like an easy enough target. Much like many disputes involving such types of men, it had involved a sum of money and a woman.

The money had been enough to bring out the worst in everyone involved, and the woman had been none other than Jennifer Dawson herself. At the time, she'd been Jennifer Grady and hadn't had her sights set completely on Bobby just yet. But that was another story.

Everything had wound up with Clint stepping in on Bobby's behalf and settling the matter as best he could. He'd left the next day, comfortable in the knowledge that he'd done the right thing. Since then, he really hadn't thought about Dawson or what had become of him.

Kelly listened to all of this and nodded. Even though Clint glazed over some of the more colorful aspects of what had happened, she seemed so concerned about the people in his story that Clint was beginning to think that she'd actually known them.

"So this poor man was killed," Kelly said while shaking her head. If anything, she seemed to have even more remorse in her face as she reached out to brush her hand along Clint's shoulder soothingly.

Sometimes, after seeing so much death and chaos in his own travels, Clint forgot how hardened he'd become to them. To most people, shootings and gunfights were not a normal part of their lives. As silly as it might sound, that kind of excitement was relatively rare to those who weren't The Gunsmith.

Clint felt bad about Bobby Dawson getting killed and he fully intended to go to the funeral, but he had to admit that he was relieved that it wasn't something worse. Judging by the look that had been on Kelly's face when he'd first opened the door, he was expecting something much worse or much closer to home.

"And what about his poor wife?" Kelly went on. "She must be feeling so bad. Do you think you can help her?"

"Yeah," Clint said while nodding solemnly. "I should be able to do something useful."

"When are you heading out there?"

Clint had already turned away from her and was gathering his belongings which were scattered about the room. There wasn't much. Just a change of clothes and a few toiletries. Normally, they would be stored in his saddlebags, but when he got further into the city, he carried them in a knapsack which he slung over his shoulder. "As soon as possible. By the sound of it, I doubt there's much time to spare."

"So where is Byrne?"

"In Kansas. It's east of Wichita and west of Coyville."

Clint could tell by the blank stare on Kelly's face that he might as well have pointed out some location on the surface of the moon. It just went to prove the point that, no matter how big a city it was, if a person never left it they were still just as sheltered.

Kelly furrowed her brow and cocked her head to one side before asking, "Is that around Chicago?"

The more he thought about that message, the more Clint wanted to get moving. "Yeah," he said as a way to avoid another couple minutes' worth of conversation. "It's near there."

SIX

Clint was no stranger to death. With killers gunning for him for no better reason than his name, he'd gotten used to the fact that death was something he just needed to deal with. Like sickness or hunger, it wasn't a great part of life, but something that happened all the same. And also like those other things, a man learned to deal with it and avoid it at all costs rather than be dominated and eventually destroyed by it.

Not only did Clint have to deal with the fact that men out in the world wanted him dead, he also had to come to terms with the fact that he had to kill other men himself. And if that weren't already enough, the people around him were sometimes lost as well.

Here, Clint wasn't thinking about innocent victims or women and children. He was thinking about the gamblers, gunfighters and lawmen that traveled in many of his own circles. Those men knew the risks just as well as Clint did. Sometimes they caught up with Clint in a saloon over a round of drinks . . . and sometimes Clint went to visit them before they were lowered into the ground.

As soon as the train had pulled away from the New York City station, Clint found his seat, waved one last time to Kelly, who stood on the platform, and then sat back to start thinking about what was ahead. One of the first things on his mind was what Bobby Dawson had done this time to call down the thunder.

Last time, he'd tried to take the money right out from under a killer's nose. The cash had been rightfully his; otherwise Clint wouldn't have stepped in on his side. But it was one of those situations that could have been easily avoided if one side could have just swallowed his pride and walked away.

So many fights could be avoided that way. So many men would still be alive if they could just slow their pace for a bit and let the trouble blow right past them. Dawson was a proud man and knew his rights. Not only that, but he often made sure to tell everyone and anyone around him what those rights were . . . loudly.

Bobby Dawson was a good man, but he was impetuous, outspoken, and had a knack for stirring up trouble. Not all of his business ventures were on the right side of the law, but he was still basically a good man. In the wrong company, that could be a downright lethal combination. Clint shook his head as he stared out the window and thought about the time he'd spent helping Dawson. The man would fight for what he believed and stick to his guns until the bitter end.

Unfortunately, it seemed as though he'd finally reached that bitter end and left a good woman to dress in black and cry in his name.

Death no longer surprised Clint Adams.

Death didn't even trouble him as much as it used to.

For that, Clint was a little upset, that his circumstances could rob him of that innocence.

He had plenty of time to think on that train to Coyville, and in the first several hours of that time, Clint thought about the reason he was riding those rails in the first place.

Someone had reached out to him in a time of need. A man who'd called him friend was dead.

There were respects to be paid and debts to settle. Knowing what he knew about Bobby Dawson, Clint was certain that there was something more going on than just a simple stray bullet or mindless brawl. The fact that his widow didn't go into the circumstances only drove that notion further home.

Even as he sat in that seat, Clint could still remember the crafty grin Bobby wore whenever he thought he was pulling off something particularly clever. Since Clint had only known the man a short amount of time and was already familiar with that grin, he knew that Bobby must have been pulling off a lot of clever things. Well . . . clever in his own mind, anyway.

As the trip had worn on and the days wound down, Clint thought less and less about what might have happened to Bobby. He didn't bother, since doing so would only wind him up tighter than the watch in his pocket. He'd sat back, looked out the window, talked to his neighbors and watched the scenery flow by.

The telegram remained folded in his jacket pocket and his jacket remained folded in a compartment over his seat. On the long trip across the country, it was easy to forget about where he'd started. The days had a way of moving that was so slow, it got to the point where Clint swore he'd been traveling for a solid month.

His seat became his home, and the few passengers that were traveling as far as he were his only friends. And when the conductor slammed the door at the front of the car on his way to the next one in line, Clint felt as though he'd been woken up from a long, restless sleep.

"Next stop . . . Byrne."

The words still drifted through the stuffy confines of the passenger car even after the man who'd spoken them had gone. Clint looked out the window and saw that the sun was starting to sink below the horizon. If the train was still on schedule and the conductor's estimation could be trusted, they would be arriving in a few hours.

The end of the line for that particular locomotive was in Dodge City, a little ways west. Realizing that he'd taken the train almost all the way as far as it was going to go, Clint felt even more tired than he'd felt the entire trip. He stared out the window and studied the flat, seemingly endless plains. He felt as though he was already in the saddle of his black Darley Arabian stallion, Eclipse, with the fresh open air surrounding him on all sides.

The horse was in the livestock car along with a few others who were accompanying their riders over the steel trail. It was nice to cover so much ground in so little time, but Clint was getting anxious to follow his own trail once again.

If he could, he would have liked to try and sleep through what little remained of his trip. But there was no way he could close his eyes now that he was almost at his destination. Now, like they had at the beginning of his trip, his thoughts were circling around Bobby Dawson, his wife, and the letter still folded in his jacket pocket.

Plenty of questions had been fermenting inside his brain throughout the long train ride. Hopefully, some of the answers he was after were waiting for him at the next station.

SEVEN

The heat of Kansas in the summertime was like a creature that kept strictly to the plains. Although anyone who spent a fair amount of time out of doors became accustomed to such things, it would take a man without any nerves in his skin not to notice the difference between the clammy, stifling humidity of the South and the drier summers of the Southwest, which gave a man a taste of what it was like to be baked in an oven.

Stepping off the train, even with the sun reduced to a golden sliver in the western sky, Clint was immediately reminded of just how distinctive a prairie summer truly was. Compared to the heat he'd left behind on the East Coast, what he felt as his boots touched down onto Byrne soil was more reminiscent of the waves that rose up from a smoldering campfire.

The air didn't stick to his skin like it did in Missouri or Louisiana. The winds weren't as heavy as the ones that blew in from the Atlantic and through the streets of New York City. Instead, Kansas felt . . . calm. Hot . . . yes. Dry . . . certainly. But still calm, all the same.

The change felt good to Clint. With the summer dragging on and heading toward its hottest months, it was going to be nice to spend them in a place where the shade could offer some comfort. When the air was thick and humid, it stuck to you no matter where you went. When Clint pulled in a lungful of the Kansas air, he didn't feel any of it clinging to his skin. It simply washed over him and kept going.

It was nice.

"Clint? Is that you, Clint Adams?"

Hearing his name shouted across the platform was more than enough to snap him out of his contemplations on the weather. Clint turned to look in the direction where the voice had come from, doing his best to get himself back on his normal mental track. After spending the last several days sitting in a box rolling across country, it was awfully easy to get lost inside one's own head.

Rubbing his eyes and hiking his warbag a little higher onto his shoulder, Clint stepped away from the train so he could separate himself from the flow of people trying to go through the doors. The engine's whistle sounded, washing out the voices which all mingled together on the platform.

Finally, after the whistle's shrill cry faded away, Clint could hear that same voice from a few moments ago.

"Over here, Clint!"

Since he'd left New York City in such a rush, Clint had nearly forgotten about sending a telegram in reply to the one he'd gotten from Bobby's widow, Jennifer. He was lucky to get aboard the train less than an hour before it was set to depart. Otherwise, he would have had to wait for another couple days before making the trip across the country.

As it wound up, Clint made his train but couldn't wait around for any sort of reply to his own telegram. Therefore, he hadn't had his hopes up that there would be anyone at the station to greet him when he arrived. It seemed that everyone was wrong sometimes.

It had been a while since Clint had last seen Jennifer. She had a pretty face and friendly eyes. Her long, black hair had a natural curl to it that gave her a more youthful appearance that many women envied. Her skin was smooth and her body was just the right kind of plump that made her soft and nice to hold.

The years of married life had added a few pounds to her, but she was still unmistakable. Clint recognized her the moment she came walking through the crowd. Her hair was longer as well and the black dress she wore was conservative, but it was still unable to hide her generous curves.

"Hello, Jen," Clint said as he opened his arms. "It's good to see you again."

Her eyes were still as warm as ever. The instant she saw Clint acknowledge her greeting, she rushed forward and threw herself into his arms. Tears were streaming down her face, and for the next couple seconds she just held onto Clint with all the strength she could muster.

Clint patted her on the back and held her until he felt her grip loosen just a bit. From there, he took a step back and put both his hands on her shoulders. "It's been a while. Let me get a look at you."

Lowering her face and dabbing at the tear streaks on it, Jen managed to smile a bit. "I'm a mess, Clint. Not like the last time you saw me."

"You look great, Jen," he said, meaning every word. Despite the sadness of their circumstances, Clint couldn't help but think back to when he'd last shared a lot of time with Jennifer. Her embrace just now had brought it all back. She still felt warm and soft in his arms. In fact, she felt even stronger now, more like a woman than the young lady he'd left behind.

She smiled up at him. The tears seemed to have stopped and her smile faded just a bit. "You're not too bad your-self." It was obvious by the look in her eyes that she was thinking back to old times as well. She blinked those thoughts away, however, and cleared her throat. "Clint Adams, I'd like you to meet a friend of mine . . ."

It wasn't until that very moment that Clint even noticed the other woman standing behind and to the side of Jennifer. She'd been keeping a respectful distance with her hands clasped in front of her. When she saw Jen turn in her direction, the other woman stepped forward and offered a hand and a smile to Clint.

"This is Shannon Carsey," Jen said. "Shannon's a good friend of mine and she hasn't left my side since . . ." Jen's face darkened and her voice caught in the back of her throat. Once again, she cleared her throat and tried to push on. "Well . . . since all of the unpleasantness lately."

Shannon was taller than Jennifer, standing a few inches higher than her friend and an inch or so shorter than Clint. She appeared to be slightly younger than Jen, with a similar body type. Her hair was a chestnut shade of brown and was much straighter than Jen's, hanging down to just past her shoulders. Her skin was darker, reflecting a combination of a Mediterranean heritage mixed with more time spent in the sun.

"How do you do," Shannon said, waiting for Clint to take the hand she was offering.

Clint held her hand and squeezed it once. Her skin wasn't quite as smooth as Jen's, but there was a different kind of strength inside of her that was shown in her confident stride and the way she locked her eyes onto his own. "Pleased to meet you. I'm sorry we had to meet under such grave circumstances."

"Me too. From what Jen was telling me about you, you're quite the man to know."

Clint glanced over to Jen with a subtle raise of his eyebrow. Wondering what, exactly, Jen had told her, he tried to get a hint from Jen's face. Unfortunately, she'd chosen that moment to glance at something else happening at the other end of the platform.

Sensing that Jen wasn't about to come clean just yet, Clint looked back to Shannon and said, "Nothing too bad I hope."

Shannon smirked. "No. Nothing bad at all." She said those words in just such a way that made Clint start to worry.

"Well, I've got to fetch my horse before he winds up riding all the way to Wichita. They should be unloading right about now." He looked at Jen once more and saw that she was still staring off at the other end of the platform.

At first, he'd been thinking that she was just trying to keep from blushing in his face. Now, however, Clint saw that something else had caught her attention. Some*one* else, actually.

There were three of them, and not only were they armed, but they were headed straight for the frightened widow.

EIGHT

The three men walked with steam in their strides that seemed to come from the fire burning in their eyes. Even from the other end of the platform, with most of the length of the train separating them, Clint could make out that look and could tell that it was trained directly upon the widow of Bobby Dawson.

"Come over here," Clint said to Jen while reaching out to take her by the wrist and pull her back.

She stumbled slightly, but not from Clint tugging her back. Jen already seemed shaky on her feet and was immediately responsive to having someone step in and tell her what to do. Shannon seemed plenty nervous as well, but didn't need to be told a word to know that Clint's invitation extended to her as well.

Both women moved back, allowing Clint to step forward and get between them and the approaching trio of armed men. Those other three were only a few cars' lengths away and had already picked up their pace. Behind them, the livestock car was being unloaded by a pair of men working from a list of passengers scheduled to pick up their animals at that stop.

"Do you know them?" Clint asked.

"Yes" was Jen's shaky reply.

"Are they the reason you called me?"

There was a moment of silence from the women behind him. When it was broken, it was Shannon who answered Clint's question.

"They're part of the problem," the other woman said. "But they were only sent by the man who's causing all the trouble here. Mr. Prowler would rather send his dogs to do his dirty work for him. Especially when he thinks there might be someone else involved besides a couple women."

The three men were only a car's length away by then. Having spotted Clint as the one protecting the two women, they were slowing down a bit and talking to each other in quick, hushed sentences. Although their heads turned slightly to speak and listen, they never took their eyes off of Clint, and the fire inside them only seemed to burn a little brighter.

With the train hissing idly beside him, Clint settled his hands on his hips in a way that shielded more of the two women behind him with his own body. He waited until the trio walked up and stopped about ten feet in front of him. "Can I help you men with something?" he asked.

All of the men glared at Clint with narrowed eyes and sneers pasted across their mouths. All of them were of roughly average height and build. Despite the scruff on their faces, not a one of them could have passed for a day over twenty-three years old. Two of them were dressed like farmhands sporting gun belts, but the one in the middle had on a brown vest over a tan shirt.

Apparently, the one with the slightly better clothes was the leader, since he was the one who spoke up first. "Who the hell are you?" he asked, wearing a scowl designed to put fear into Clint's soul.

Although the young man's bad look had less effect on Clint than a snarl from a scared puppy, he decided to keep that fact to himself for the moment. There was no need to lay down all of his cards just then.

Clint kept his face steady, with a little hint of weariness mixed in to keep the trio thinking they were the ones in the driver's seat. He wasn't much of an actor, but with the grueling train ride still fresh in his bones, weariness wasn't exactly tough to pull off. Judging by the smug looks on the three kids' faces, he did a good enough job to convince them.

"He asked you a question, mister," one of the two farm-hands said. "You'd best answer before we toss you under this here train as it's rolling out." Apparently, he'd bought into what Clint was selling hook, line and sinker.

"I'm just trying to visit with some friends of mine," Clint said. "Is there a law against that?"

The one in the vest cocked his head to one side and stood with his shoulders and feet squared off. "No. But there is a law against what we can do to you if you decide to stand in our way. Too bad the lawmen here don't have the sand to enforce it."

Clint took a quick look around by shifting his eyes slightly in either direction. He wanted to get a feel for his surroundings, but knew better than to let the three men in front of him out of his sight. First in his mind was to make sure that there weren't too many other people on the platform around him.

As far as that went, he could see some others watching the scene, but none of them had the inclination to stick their noses into it. That was fine by Clint, since the only ones he wanted close to him were Jen and Shannon. Both women kept behind him, letting him know they were there by keeping their hands gently touching the back of his shoulder.

Clint was also looking to see if there were any other troublemakers trying to get behind him or flank him by sneaking onto another part of the platform. Since most of the pedestrian traffic had cleared out, it would have been easy to see if that was happening. Apparently, the cocky youths were confident enough in their abilities not to use any backup. Clint highly doubted there were any snipers nearby, although he wasn't about to rule them out.

He gathered all of this information in the time it took for his eyes to twitch to one side and back again. The train's whistle sounded in two short bursts to let everyone know it was about to pull out of the station. Before Clint spoke to the arrogant kids in front of him again, he glanced over their shoulders and spotted a familiar, large black shape moving off the train.

Still certain they had the upper hand, the trio took another step forward and lowered their hands to the guns at their sides. That simple motion caused a change in Clint's mind. He looked at them as threats and potential targets after that, although his eyes reflected not even the slightest bit of difference.

"Step away from them women," the one in the vest said. "There's plenty more of 'em in the whorehouse on Ridgemont Avenue."

Clint kept his voice level and nonthreatening. "Not until I know what your intentions are."

The two farmhands looked to the one in the middle, resembling a pair of dogs begging for the word to attack.

"I'll tell you what our intentions are. We mean to make you sorry you was ever born."

NINE

Knowing that nothing was holding them back except for their own initiative, the two farmhands started moving toward Clint. They didn't just charge up to him, but instead moved subtly in place, drifting closer over a matter of seconds like wolves circling their prey. Their faces bore cruel smiles and their eyes glared hungrily at what they thought was an easy kill.

When Clint sensed that they were about to make their play, he shrugged his shoulder just enough to give them a peek at the Colt hanging at his side. They couldn't tell that the weapon was a one-of-a-kind masterpiece of his own design, but they didn't have to know that much to be certain that the game wasn't going to be quite as easy as they'd thought.

Without having to be told, Jan and Shannon moved back to give Clint room to maneuver. Shannon was somewhat reluctant at first, but Jen gave her a nod and motioned that it was all right to leave Clint on his own. Having seen him in his element before, Jen knew that all she had to do now was find a safe place to hide. Her stomach twisted with regret that things had gotten so ugly so quickly, but she'd known it was going to happen sooner or later.

Clint sized up the trio in front of him with the eyes of an expert. He watched everything from the way they moved to the way their guns were strapped around their waists. One of them wore his holster low on his hip, which was a popular way to brandish a weapon if it was for nothing else but show.

Also, the two weapons carried by the farmhands seemed shiny and gleaming in what little light there was. That either meant they were new and hardly used or polished every night before they went to bed. Clint figured the former was more likely the case, which told him that the hands wielding the weapons were probably just as new.

All three of them were coming forward. They'd already taken up positions and spread out, giving Clint more targets to shoot at. The more time went by, the higher the tension got between all four men. Every step was taken as if through a lake of molasses. Every motion was careful and calculated.

The trio of younger men seemed eager to fight, but still hesitant now that they knew their target was armed.

Clint, on the other hand, didn't even move.

He was a statue on that platform, whose eyes were the only thing that didn't seem chiseled out of stone. His hand drifted so slowly toward his Colt that the motion couldn't even be seen by the advancing youths. And although his body was solid and unmoving, every one of his muscles tensed beneath his skin, preparing for the moment that was swiftly approaching.

Once the trio had covered what little ground they needed and were set up exactly where they wanted to be, they paused for a second to look across at one another. The one in the vest nodded and looked back toward Clint.

"Last chance, mister," the kid said. "Let the bitches come with us or we'll burn you down."

Clint's only response was a subtle shake of his head.

The kid in the vest saw it well enough. "Have it your way," he said with a smug grin. "Don't say we didn't warn you."

Studying every move the trio made, Clint held still until he knew that it was absolutely necessary for him to move. So far, the trio seemed to be full of more steam than the departing engine, but that was about it. He'd been hoping, for their sakes, that they would let the matter drop after a few rounds of threats and tough talk.

But that didn't seem to be the case. Those three wanted to do things the hard way. It was unfortunate, but only for them. Clint wasn't good at doing things the hard way.

He was the best.

The first one to draw was the farmhand on Clint's left. That was the one wearing his holster slung low at the hip, which also seemed to mean that he was the one who fancied himself the deadliest of the three. His hand slapped against the side of his holster in a clumsy attempt to draw faster than he was able. By the time he finally did manage to clear leather, his finger was fumbling to slide in beneath the trigger guard.

In the time it took for all of this to happen, Clint figured he might have been able to draw and fire off three shots of his own. But he still didn't want to show everything he had just then, and so he'd waited to let the kids make their play.

Now that one of them was about to fire, Clint decided it was time to show them the difference between talk and deeds. His hand swept upward along the side of his holster, plucking the Colt from its resting place as his fingers slid around it. His gun belt was worn the proper way, placing the pistol in the prime spot for his arm and hand to draw and fire with the least amount of fuss.

The Colt barked once, spitting a single round through the air, which punched through the farmhand's rib cage and sent him spinning like a top on one foot. The kid's gun went off as well, but sent its own bullet into the ground several feet short of its target. Like most overly anxious types, he just couldn't wait to pull his trigger. Not only did that cause him to miss his target, but it also earned him a fresh wound and a quick trip off his feet.

The second farmhand was only a few seconds behind the first, having just pulled his own gun and preparing to fire. So far, the one in the vest was taking his time and only now started to draw his weapon.

"Take yer time," the one in the vest snarled. "Just shoot the woman if you have to."

Clint reflexively shot a glance over his shoulder to see where Jen and Shannon had gone. He couldn't see them right away, which meant that they were at least safe from the gunfire for the moment. Unfortunately, it also meant that his suspicions had been confirmed.

He'd taken his eyes off of his attackers.

In doing so, he'd broken one of the cardinal rules of gunfighting. Not only that, but he'd fallen for one of the oldest tricks in the book. With two women under his protection, however, he couldn't afford to take the chance that they were really about to get shot.

Now . . . he was about to pay for that concern.

Clint spun back around with his gun up and ready. Even though he didn't have the other two in his sights again, he instinctively ducked down as he twisted around. Dropping to one knee as he completed the turn, Clint looked as if he'd screwed his leg into the boards of the platform while a pair of shots whipped through the air over his head.

From the corner of one eye, Clint saw a hint of movement, followed by a rumble and grinding sound. The train was starting to move away, and soon he felt a blast of steam wash over him from behind.

The second farmhand took another shot. This time, he was starting to panic and the round went wide to chip through the glass of one of the train's windows. A scream sounded from inside the locomotive as another pair of shots blasted through the air.

Those shots came from the kid in the vest as well as the farmhand that Clint had put down. The poorly dressed gunman was hurt and clamping a hand to the bloody wound in his side, but was still struggling to do his job.

Both of the shooters that were still standing had gotten closer together and appeared to be coordinating their shots. With the women still in need of protection and no cover to be found, Clint was left with few other choices but to play his trump card and unleash his full speed. In doing so, he might as well have sent a telegram of his own to the rest of Byrne's gunmen, telling them that he was a force to be reckoned with.

That same message would almost certainly be Jennifer's death warrant.

TEN

It would only be a matter of seconds before one of the young killers got in a lucky shot. The only way to prevent that was to drop both of them. Then again, Clint figured there just might be another way to keep from entering town on the tail of three killings.

And so, before taking his next shot, Clint put his fingers to his lips and blew a shrill, piercing whistle.

The act seemed strange enough at the time for all three of the shooters to stop for a second to take notice. Besides marking them as even greener than Clint had thought, it added an extra second or two for Clint's plan to take effect.

"What the hell is he doin'?" the wounded farmhand asked as he struggled to take another shot.

The one in the vest shook his head and sighted down the length of his barrel. "I don't give a damn what he's doin'. Just drop him so we can get to that woman."

The other two didn't have a problem with that and were well on their way to carrying out those orders when another sound caught their attention. This time, however, the sound didn't come from Clint. It didn't even come from

Clint's end of the platform. Instead, it was coming from behind them.

It wasn't just the sound that caught their attention, but the slight quaking that rippled through the floorboards like a tremor. The wood slats rattled beneath the shooters' feet in a rhythm that reminded them of huge, drumming fingers.

The drumming rattled in a series of four quick beats, a quick pause and then four more beats. That was all the time the shooters needed before they looked over their shoulders to see what could be making such a racket. When they turned around, they were just in time to see something huge and dark looming over them, eclipsing the sky like a speeding storm front passing overhead.

Clint watched as the familiar dark shape from the other end of the platform took notice of his whistle and responded without the slightest hesitation. The big Darley Arabian stallion's ears had pricked up at the call of his master and came running.

The horse's hooves pounded against the boards, carrying it to within a few feet of the trio's position. That was about the time when they'd turned around to look, and the stallion launched himself into the air and over the shooters' heads, clearing them as though they were a low bar in a steeplechase.

"Holy sh—" was all the kid in the vest had a chance to say before Eclipse nearly knocked his head clean off his shoulders.

The stallion landed in front of the shooters and trotted over to where Clint was waiting. He shook his mane and whinnied as if greeting his master after being separated throughout the long, grueling train ride.

Clint stepped around the horse and took aim at the three shooters before they could regain their bearings after the near-miss. By the looks of it, they seemed to have been shaken up just enough to suit his purposes.

"Toss away those guns," Clint said. "Make it quick."

The wounded farmhand was the first to oblige. Not only was he hurting from the bullet buried in his side, but he'd emptied every one of his chambers in a blind panic to return fire. He pitched the gun as though the steel burnt his hands, laying his head and hands down onto the platform.

The second farmhand had run out of steam as well. He looked at the one in the vest for less than a second and then glanced back to Clint. As soon as he saw the modified Colt already pointing directly at him, the youth spat out a curse and let his own pistol slide out from his fingers.

"Jesus Christ," the one in the vest proclaimed. "Nothin' but a sorry bunch of chicken shits. I should've never let you work for me and Mr. Prowler."

"I'm not gonna tell you again," Clint warned.

"You can tell it till you're blue in the face, old man. Next you can tell it to your maker."

Clint waited through the kid's tough talk and kept his eyes trained on the youth's face. There was a certain way a man set his jaw and cinched in the skin around his eyes before he was about to pull the trigger. There wasn't a good way to explain it, but Clint recognized it as the best way to know when the lead was about to fly.

When he saw that face on someone facing him down, he knew he had about a second before he had to defend himself.

The kid in the vest strutted forward and locked his eyes on Clint. Then, his face turned into the very mask that Clint had been waiting for as he jerked his gun hand up and began squeezing his trigger.

Clint's arm barely twitched. Using as little effort as possible, he pointed and fired before the kid got a chance to throw out his next insult. The Colt barked once and the kid felt a pinching in his chest.

There were two more impacts against the platform. First, the kid's gun clattered against the boards. Next, the kid himself dropped flat on his back to bleed out through the fresh hole in his heart.

ELEVEN

Clint looked around and waited a moment to see if there were any more men still to come from the deadly welcoming committee. If there were, they'd decided to fight another day, because the only people left on the platform were frightened civilians and a few stunned railroad workers.

Once he'd dropped the Colt back into his holster, Clint spotted Jen and Shannon hiding behind a pile of crates and luggage. Also at that time, he saw an old man running with an awkward limp that turned nearly every one of his steps into a stumble. The old man had a head of shaggy gray hair and a mustache that looked like a weed, which had overgrown his mouth.

"What's goin' on here?" the old man said.

Before Clint could say anything, he heard Jen's voice whispering to him as she walked out from where she'd been hiding.

"That's Sheriff Larkins," she said. "He's always late for the scuffles when Mr. Prowler's men are involved."

"You want to know what happened?" Clint said to the sheriff. "Then you'd best ask them two over there. While you're at it . . . ask any of the people that were on this platform."

The old man walked up to Clint, wheezing even when he came to a stop next to Eclipse. "Seein' as there's a dead man laying over there, I'm sure you'll understand if I ask you to stay here for a moment or two and tell me what happened yourself."

After the grueling train ride and the reception he'd gotten upon arrival at his destination, Clint's first inclination was to turn his back on the lawman and head straight for the nearest hotel. It wasn't as if the dead man wouldn't be dead in the morning.

But as much as he tried to fight it back, Clint's sense of responsibility prevented him from doing what his baser instincts so desperately wanted. He didn't know for a fact if Sheriff Larkins was crooked or not. A badge was a badge, and until he knew any different, he was accustomed to helping the enforcers of the law rather than snubbing them.

"All right, Sheriff," Clint said. "I'll tell you what happened, but don't you think you should be taking the guns from those men over there first?"

"I should be taking yours as well," Larkins replied. "In fact, maybe you should hand it over while I—"

"No need for that, Sheriff."

The person who'd spoken up was a well-dressed banker with a waxed mustache and hair parted neatly down the middle. Clint knew he was a banker because he'd sat across from the other man for the better part of two days during the train ride from New York. The banker had been the kind who prattled on and on about nothing, but he seemed like a decent enough sort.

"I saw the whole thing," the banker said. "It was self-defense. Those three men came up and were threatening these here ladies."

The sheriff caught his breath and nodded quickly. "That

may be the case, but I'm still gonna have to—"

"I saw it too." This time, it was a young woman who stepped forward. She'd also been on the train and was standing by the fiancé she'd described to Clint no fewer than a dozen times on the train. The fiancé nodded as well.

"Clint's here on my behalf," Jen said. "Shannon and I were nearly killed by these dogs on Prowler's payroll."

It looked as though the sheriff was about to say something else, but he stopped when he saw Shannon step forward and look into his eyes. She actually stood at eye level with Larkins and smiled warmly as she started to speak.

"Thanks for coming here, Sheriff," she said softly. "I feel so much safer now that you came to cage them up like the animals they are. You don't really have to treat Clint the same way, do you? He stood up for us just like you would have done if you were here."

Larkins drew in a deep breath and propped both hands upon his hips. His back straightened amid a series of wet pops, and the corners of his mustache curled up into a proud grin. "I guess there's no reason to detain your friend. Not with all these witnesses speaking on his behalf." Turning to Clint, he put on a stern expression and added, "But you'd better not be leaving town anytime soon. I might still want to have a word with you later on."

Clint nodded. "Of course, Sheriff. I understand."

Wheeling around to face the two remaining thugs, Larkins placed his hand on the butt of his gun and stalked forward. "Get up, you two. Kick them guns over to me."

Wounded, scared and defeated, the two farmhands did as best they could. One had to help up the other, who was still bleeding profusely from the wound in his side. All the fight was out of them, however. That was plain enough for anyone to see.

"You," Larkins said while jabbing a finger toward the healthier of the two shooters. "Carry that other one to the doc's office. I'll be right behind you and then I'll escort you back here to drag that other one to the undertaker's."

The kid started to talk back, but didn't have the breath left to form the words. Also, a glare from Clint bowed the younger man's head and caused him to start in on his appointed tasks.

Clint walked up to each of the people who'd spoken up for him and thanked them in turn. Until they'd raised their voices, he was certain they were all long gone. But when he expressed his thanks to them, they waved it off and said that they were only telling the truth.

"Well, the truth's worth a drink on me. Or maybe dinner if you're in town for a while," he said to them.

Both the banker and the young woman nodded and accepted his offer. Once Sheriff Larkins had taken away the two young men, nobody seemed much inclined to stick around the station any longer.

"Looks like the place is clearing out," Shannon said.

Clint took hold of Eclipse's reins and started to walk away from the tracks as well. "That's not a bad idea. I have a feeling the sheriff might not be so generous if it wasn't for some of your persuasion on my behalf."

Shannon grinned and batted her eyelashes. "Why, I swear I have no idea what you mean."

Laughing, Clint said, "All right, you can hold off on the feminine wiles. I might not be as easy to sway as some lonely old man."

"Sure," Jen said as she fell into step with them. "That's what Sheriff Larkins said before he wound up wrapped around her little finger."

TWELVE

Jen led the way once they were off the train platform. It was plain to see that Byrne had grown a bit since the last time Clint had visited the town. Where there had once been just a platform built along the side of the train tracks, there was now a small depot as well, complete with a small telegraph office attached on one side.

The platform emptied out onto Ridgemont Avenue, just as it had before, except this time the street was a little more crowded. There was another saloon as well as several other buildings where there had previously been nothing but open prairie and shoddy houses. There were more people as well, milling about and standing around, most of them waiting to see who'd been causing all the shooting minutes ago.

"This town seems to be prospering," Clint said.

Jen hooked her arm through his and nodded. "It's been thriving since the railroad came. Last time you were here, we didn't even have a station."

"That's right. I think the rails were still clean."

"True enough. They'd just been built through here right before you met up with . . . ," she paused and lowered her head as some of the darkness in her manner returned, ". . . before you met up with Bobby."

They'd turned right once they stepped onto the street, and she led him to a livery that was right next to the train station. Clint stopped there and took Jen in his arms. She embraced him immediately and started to cry. Her shoulders shook as the sobs began exploding from her.

"Oh Clint," she said once she could catch her breath. "Things have been so terrible since my Bobby died. That man Prowler made our lives miserable when Bobby was alive and now that he's gone, he expects to just march in and take what he thinks is his.

"I was going to just give him whatever he wanted, but then I thought that Bobby would have been so disappointed in me. If I did that, he would've died for nothing. I could never thank you enough for coming all the way from New York City to help me."

Clint had plenty of questions for her, but he knew that this wasn't the time to ask them. So instead, he nodded and wiped away some of her tears with his thumb. "Try not to worry so much, Jen. I'm here now."

Doing her best to smile through the tears, she looked up at him and said, "I know you are. That makes me feel so much better."

It wasn't long before Jen pulled herself together and dug around in her handbag for a kerchief to dry her eyes and cheeks. Clint remembered her as a woman who had strong opinions but was relatively frail in many ways. She needed someone to stand with her and support her when things got hard. She was the kind of woman who looked to someone else before relying on her own fortitude.

Already, Clint noticed a difference in her. Now that she'd been widowed, it seemed as though she was used to hardship and was developing more inner strength. After all, she'd seen the death of her husband as well as these other men coming after her with guns. When something like that happens to a person, they had two choices: adjust or collapse.

Fortunately, Jen appeared to be doing her level best to adjust to her new situation. She wasn't alone, however. Already, Shannon was moving in to wrap an arm around her and offer soft, soothing words of comfort. Shannon looked up at Clint and nodded toward the livery, letting him know that she could take care of Jen while he tended to his horse.

The livery consisted of only three stalls. Fortunately, two of those were empty and the fee for renting one was well within reason. Once Clint had Eclipse squared away, he stepped out to rejoin the two women waiting for him on the street.

Jen had stopped crying and took a deep breath to collect herself when she saw Clint emerge from the livery.

"My house is right down this street," she said. "I've got some pies cooling and a roast that should be done before too long."

"Those wouldn't be the peach pies that you used to make when I was here last time, would they?"

Beside him, Shannon started to laugh. "I thought you didn't spend too much time here, Mr. Adams."

"It wasn't a long stay, but it sure was an eventful one. And I doubt I'd forget about Jen's peach pie even if I was dead."

The conversation remained on such common topics as favorite desserts and the growth of Byrne. It was much easier for Jennifer to keep her spirits up that way, so Clint was more than happy to oblige. It didn't take them long to reach the end of the street, which was also the end of the boardwalk.

At the edge of town the street opened up into a residential area, with homes built side by side in a roughly square-shaped pattern. Most of the homes were two floors high, with small picket fences separating one yard from another. Townspeople sat in rockers on the little porches and waved as Clint and the two ladies strolled by.

Although Clint noticed so many ways that the town of Byrne had grown, the place also struck him as being so very small. Most of that could be attributed to having come straight out of one of the biggest cities in the world and shot across the country into the heart of Kansas.

Byrne was a far cry from New York City in so many ways. In fact, the town could probably fit in one or two of the city's blocks. But the air in Byrne was so much cleaner and the sky stretched out over Clint's head like a vast tapestry of stars and clouds. Also, a home like the one that Jen stepped up to would be awfully hard to find within the teeming masses of New York City.

"Here we are," the widow said as she climbed the narrow stairs onto her porch. "The house is pretty much the same as the last time you were here. Bobby might have put on a coat of paint since then, but otherwise it's still the same."

Clint followed her inside and Shannon brought up the rear, closing the door behind them. The air inside the comfortable home was hot and smelled of the cooling dessert Jen had promised.

Heading straight for the kitchen, Jen reached for an apron hanging from a hook on the wall and tied it around her waist. "Supper should be ready in a bit. Can I get you something to drink?"

Nodding, Clint said, "That sounds—"

"Fine," Shannon interrupted. "That sounds just fine, but I'm sure Mr. Adams could use something stronger than lemonade after all he's been through. What with the long trip and all the trouble at the station, I'll bet he could use something to calm his nerves."

Clint was thinking that some lemonade and a slice of pie would be just what he needed to relax. But when he looked over to Shannon, he got an insistent nod and a pleading stare. "I could use something to take the edge off."

Jen peeked around from the kitchen. "Sorry, but I don't keep anything too strong in the house after . . . well . . . maybe Shannon could take you to the Sundowner for a drink."

"I'll do that," Shannon said, taking Clint by the hand and leading him toward the front door. "We won't be long."

"All right then. Be sure to hurry back."

Once they were outside, Clint stopped in his tracks and turned to look at Shannon. "What was that all about?"

"I wanted to talk to you alone. There's some things I need to tell you, and they're not the sort of things that Jen needs to hear right now."

"All right. Come to think of it, I've got some questions of my own."

THIRTEEN

The Sundowner was a saloon on Ridgemont Avenue right across from a blacksmith's shop. It had been a while since Clint had been in a town so small that it didn't even have a scandalous district. The closest Byrne could come was the saloon, which was right next to a social club, which just so happened to be frequented by plenty of women who spent a lot of time sitting on the front porch in their slips.

Shannon led Clint up the street to the Sundowner in a matter of minutes. She didn't seem to be in any kind of hurry. In fact, her manner and voice were more relaxed now that she was alone with him, as opposed to looking after Jen.

"So what is it you wanted to talk to me about?" Clint asked.

After a slight pause, she turned to look at him and said, "How well did you know Jen?"

"Well enough to come halfway across the country to help her. What about you?"

Shannon turned her head down slightly, allowing some of her thick brown hair to fall in front of her face. It wasn't enough to shield her from him completely, but it

51

was like a curtain had appeared from nowhere to protect her from something she'd rather not see.

"I didn't mean to sound rude," she said quietly. "It's just that she's become like a sister to me and . . . ever since Robert was killed . . . there really hasn't been anyone else to do the job."

Suddenly, Clint felt like an ass for taking the smile from Shannon's face. "To answer your question, I knew Jen fairly well. That was before she married Bobby and it didn't last too long, but we still got close enough. I knew her well enough to know that she's a good person and probably deserved better than to spend the rest of her life with someone like Robert Dawson."

When he said that last part, Clint watched Shannon closely, waiting to see what her reaction would be to his remark. Although it could have been worded a little more delicately, there was plenty of truth in what he'd said. Anyone who knew the couple at all would have seen that.

Shannon kept her head down and reached up to brush some of her hair behind her ear. Her soft, full lips were curved into a subtle smile and she nodded slowly. "Robert was a good man . . . but you're right about him. He was trouble. He was the kind of trouble that plenty of people deserve. Jen's not one of those, though."

They were standing near the saloon, close enough to hear the noises coming from inside, but far enough away to keep their conversation from those who stood milling about in front of the place. Having watched Shannon as she spoke and taken in his own comments, Clint was coming to the conclusion that he liked her. She seemed genuinely concerned for Jen's safety, but more than that, she was someone who seemed to know more about what was going on.

"What about that drink?" he said. "Now that I'm here, you got me thinking I'm thirsty."

She laughed and leaned in a little closer to him. "That

usually only works on the sheriff, but I wouldn't mind expanding my list of conquests."

Clint offered his arm, and she took it for the entire ten-foot journey onto the boardwalk and into the saloon. The front door wasn't too dissimilar from the one on Jen's house. It swung open with oiled silence and allowed Clint to look inside.

The Sundowner wasn't a big place. There were tables taking up most of the room, with a bar along the right wall. A piano sat next to a small stage toward the back, both of which were currently unoccupied. In all, there couldn't have been more than a dozen people drinking and talking at the bar and tables. Some of them were even picking at plates of food, which were served by the tall man who also tended bar.

"No card tables?" Clint observed.

Shannon led him to an empty table close to the stage. "All of them are at Nelson Hall a few doors down. They clear the place out for town meetings every month, but besides that you can play any game you can think of in there." With a wink, she added, "As long as it's poker."

Clint took a seat and placed both hands on top of the table. "My kind of town."

The bartender came up to them and swiped at some of the water and crumbs that were still on the table. He would have been able to look down on Clint if both men were standing. But since Clint was sitting down, the bar-keep towered over him and Shannon, smirking at them from beneath a thick, finely combed black mustache.

"Evening, Miss Carsey. Who's your friend?"

"My friend is very thirsty, Dale," she said, ignoring his question. "How about setting us both up with the usual?"

"Two beers it is." And with that, the barkeep turned on his heels and made his way back to the keg resting on a small table in the corner.

"She knows where the card games are and she's a beer

drinker," Clint said. "I'm starting to suspect that you're trying to turn my head after all."

"And I'd suspect that I did that the moment we met at the train station."

Clint smiled and looked into her eyes. "You know . . . I'd argue with you if you weren't completely right."

The moment sunk into both of them, leaving them feeling a little more comfortable around one another. Clint had been feeling something for her since she'd glanced up at him with those dark eyes for the first time. Of course, with a woman as beautiful as Shannon, that didn't come as any big surprise. But the more time he'd spent around her, the more time Clint wanted to spend. It had seemed odd at first that she took him away from Jen's house like that. But he would have been lying if he said he was about to reject the idea.

Once the beers were brought to their table, Shannon's mood immediately turned more serious. She took a deep breath, steeled herself with a drink, and then looked back up at Clint.

"Robert was good at stirring up trouble, Clint. You were right about that. Not only did he stir up enough to get himself killed, but I think he turned out to be the death of Jen and me as well. Now . . . maybe even you."

Clint took a drink. "We'll just have to see about that."

FOURTEEN

For such a small place, the Sundowner managed to pack in quite a crowd. Within a few minutes, every seat was taken and every spot at the bar was filled. Eventually, an old-timer with a clean scalp sat down at the piano and started plucking out a couple simple tunes.

To Clint, it seemed as though the crowd had formed almost instantaneously. One second he was thinking about what Shannon was going to say, and the next he was pulling his seat in closer to the table to avoid being knocked over by a passing local.

"This is the best place in town to talk," Shannon said. "Especially if you don't want anyone else to hear you."

Since Clint could just barely make out her voice with her sitting right in front of him, he didn't need an explanation for that. If there had been anyone on the stage, he probably wouldn't have been able to hear his own voice.

"How much longer before Jen will come looking for us?" The question was Clint's way of trying to prod Shannon a little closer to her point.

At times, she looked like she was ready to speak. At others, she seemed afraid to make eye contact. Finally, she straightened up once again and nodded to him. "We don't have much time. She doesn't like being in that house alone for very long anyway."

"Why's that? I thought she loved that house."

"She did. When Bobby was alive."

"What was he into that was so bad?" Clint asked. "I knew he did some bit of swindling, but nothing too bad. For the most part, I thought he was just full of . . ." He stopped himself there, out of respect for the dead.

"You can say it," Shannon assured him. "He was full of horse manure half the time, and the other half he was just a lot of hot air. But he was still a good man. Well . . . he tried to be. He was good to Jennifer."

"So what is this big trouble he stirred up?"

When she asked the next question, Shannon kept her voice even lower than it had been before. Clint had to sit with one elbow propped up on the table just to hear her.

"Do you know who Owen Prowler is?"

Clint shook his head. "Not before coming here. I've heard his name a few times since then, though. Why don't you tell me who he is?"

"He's the man who got the railroad to come through this town a few years ago. If it wasn't for him, Byrne might have dried up and blown away. Listening to the way some people talk about him, he's the one responsible for the rains and sunlight as well."

"Sounds like an important man."

"He's a bastard and a liar." Shannon's voice raised when she said that, which she instantly caught and tried her best to control. She looked around as if waiting for everyone to stop and throw stones at her. But if anyone else had heard her, they didn't seem to care. All the same, she lowered her eyes and scooted her chair a little closer to the table.

Clint leaned in as well. When he was that close to her, he couldn't help but take notice of the scent of her hair and the soft texture of her skin. A couple of strands grazed his face, reminding him of a butterfly's passing wing.

She spoke to him in a voice that was almost a whisper. The sound of it sent a tremor through his skin.

"Prowler got his fortune as a kidnapper," she said. "When he was younger, he used to take rich men's children or wives and hold them for ransom. But instead of asking for money, he used to ask for favors or some little bit of power."

"What do you mean?"

"He'd take a cattle baron's little girl and ask for a piece of property in return. Or maybe he would get a couple judges in his pocket for when he needed them later. I even heard about a time when he boxed up a bank robber's son and buried him in the middle of a field. To get him back, the outlaw had to promise to steer clear of a certain part of the state so Prowler could roll in and gain even more favor with the law. Ever since then, he's been trading in secrets and blackmail. I hear he collects all his information on folks like it was a business. That's how he knows how to get to 'em when he needs to . . . or who to steal away in the dead of night."

"And where did you hear all of this?"

Wearing a look on her face that was a mix of guilt and fear, she answered, "From Bobby. It was around the time when he was getting work delivering mail on a stage-coach."

Clint had to smile at that. "Delivering mail is one of the last jobs I would ever expect Bobby Dawson to have taken."

She smirked as well. "He liked to look through the letters and open the ones he thought were important. He never stole anything, but he liked to peek in on what folks were saying and what little secrets he might be able to find."

"Now *that* sounds like the Bobby Dawson I remember."

"Bobby wasn't an honest man," Shannon said after taking another sip of her beer. "But he wasn't a bad man, either."

"If he'd had the guts to use a gun, he would have been a true hell-raiser," Clint said. "Being fidgety was the only thing keeping him on the right side of the law. Well . . . toward the right side, anyway. He had a good heart. That's why I helped him out."

"I've heard about you from Jen." Shannon paused and averted her eyes for a minute as though she suddenly felt embarrassed. "But every time Bobby talked about you, it was a different story. What kind of mess was he in?"

"Just the kind of mess you would have expected from him. He stepped a bit out of line and got the wrong people upset at him. It didn't seem like much at first, but things got out of hand and those wrong people wouldn't listen to reason. I just stepped in to smooth things out."

Shannon grinned and took another sip. "That's not half as exciting as the way he told it. He said there were bullets flying and danger around every corner."

"It's all in the way you look at it. I guess it could be seen that way. Sometimes my life feels enough like a yellowback novel. At least things could be a little calmer when I look back at them."

"If only I had that problem. If my life were any kind of book, I don't think even I'd want to read it."

"You know what they say. Be careful what you wish for."

FIFTEEN

Their beers were draining away, and both Clint and Shannon were starting to feel like they were running out of time before Jen would miss them. Also, the Sundowner was filling up to bursting and the rumble of feet behind the stage's curtain could be heard. Before too long, the possibility of a quiet, relaxed conversation inside the saloon's walls would be out of the question.

"So let me guess," Clint said after downing the last of his drink. "Bobby got his job peeking through some mail and found something that he shouldn't have."

"That's right."

"Something involving this Mr. Prowler who's so important here in town."

"Right again."

"What did he find?"

Shannon started to answer and then stopped. She looked at Clint and then lowered her eyes so that she was staring down into the glass in front of her. "You know . . . I'm not even sure."

"Great. If you just wanted to have a drink with me, you could've just asked, you know."

"Bobby was going to tell me the night he was . . ." She

lowered her voice again and moved her chair around so that she was sitting directly beside Clint. Leaning so that she could whisper into his ear, she said, "It was the night he was killed."

Suddenly, Clint became interested in the conversation once again. "You were there?"

Shannon nodded. "I don't think they saw me. If they did, they probably thought I was Jennifer. But just to be sure, they've been threatening both of us ever since. I wanted to talk to you alone for a couple reasons. First of all, Jen's got enough to worry about without hearing all of this again. She knows she's in danger and has been having a hard enough time trying to go on day to day.

"Secondly, she doesn't know everything that I know. I've been keeping some things to myself because if any of the wrong people in town knew what I saw, then Prowler wouldn't be wasting any more time in trying to kill us. He'd gun us down or even burn us up inside our own homes."

"He's done things like that?"

Again, Shannon nodded. This time, however, she seemed to be suspicious of every other soul inside the saloon. She flinched whenever an eye was turned in her direction, and she kept her shoulders bunched up around her ears with nervous tension. "Prowler's got free rein in Byrne. It's just like I told you about how he got to be so prosperous. One of the deals he made was to get immunity for himself from the law. I don't know how far it stretches, but it sure works in these parts."

Even though he wasn't as wound up as Shannon seemed to be, Clint couldn't help but be affected by her nervousness. He found himself leaning closer as well, not only to hear better, but to fit in with the way she was sitting. The tension radiated off of Shannon so strongly that Clint could feel it like fingers tickling his skin.

"If this is something that might happen to her, don't you think Jen ought to know about it?"

"You're right, Clint . . . but something else that I couldn't say in front of her is that . . . I think . . ."

Clint was certain the woman couldn't get any more nervous. When she started in trying to say her next sentence, however, he was proven wrong. Her voice started to tremble, and her eyes reflected such fear that Clint instinctively reached out to cover her hand with his own.

"Go on and say it while we're both still here," Clint urged. "If it was important enough to go through all this trouble, then you shouldn't stop before you've said your piece. Besides . . . you know I came all this way to see if I could help."

Shannon looked deeply into Clint's eyes. She wasn't just looking *at* him, but seemed to be staring at something *inside* of him as well. She stared for a few seconds and finally let out the breath she'd been holding. "I think Jennifer knows something that she doesn't want to tell anyone. I'm not sure exactly what it is, but I know it's something important, otherwise she would have told me about it by now."

"If you're not sure, how do you know there's anything for her to keep from you?"

"I've caught her a couple times hiding something when she thought I wasn't looking. And there's been once or twice when I've come to her house a little early and seen her rushing to keep me from seeing something. She says that it's nothing or that I just startled her, but something tells me that there's more to it than that."

SIXTEEN

Clint wasn't sure if he was just tired from the train ride or if more of Shannon's uneasiness was rubbing off on him. It seemed as though the saloon was getting more crowded by the second and that all of the locals were staring over at him at one point or another. Although that wouldn't have been too strange considering he was a new face in such a small town, Clint swore he was picking up on something more sinister than just simple curiosity from those other eyes.

Just to be sure, Clint returned a few of those stares to see if he could get a feel for the people behind them. He might have been a good judge of character, but even he didn't expect to see too much with such a cursory glance. Then again, what he was looking for was rather simple.

There was a certain way someone would turn away from another's eyes if they were particularly set on not meeting them. Also, there was a forced kind of nonchalance when someone would look back at him, too. As Clint looked around the room, he thought of those things and came to one definite conclusion.

Shannon's nervousness was absolutely rubbing off on him.

He took another sip of beer and turned his attention back to the woman sitting in front of him. Since she was the one who wanted to talk and she'd been the one to go to such lengths to get him away from Jen's home, then she was also the one that was most likely to let him in on what was going on.

Rather than buy completely into what Shannon was telling him just yet, Clint decided to get some of his own questions answered.

"How good friends are you?" he asked.

She put her fingertips to her temples and started rubbing as though she'd just gotten a bad headache. "We're very close. I thought we were the best of friends. She's opened up to me so much ever since all this terrible business has started. She tells me everything because there really isn't anyone else for her to turn to.

"I'm the only one who she knows won't talk to Mr. Prowler." Suddenly, she dropped her hands so she could see Clint better. "Did you hear about the reward?"

Clint shook his head.

"That awful man's put a price on any information anyone might have concerning him or his business. It's been a standing offer since he came to Byrne and set up shop. He pays well, too, which is why he always knows everything that goes on in this town." Her eyes darted back and forth as suspicion crept back into her face. "I don't even know who I can trust."

"Don't get too edgy, Shannon. That's exactly what someone who made an offer like that would want. Obviously, this Mr. Prowler has made a good living by playing people against each other. He really wouldn't need too many informants in a town this size. Just think about how much a few old ladies in the sewing circles know about everyone."

Shannon laughed at that and nodded slowly. "That's true."

"What else can you tell me about this thing that Jen's hiding from you?"

"I saw her stashing it away once in her sitting room. She was standing by a bookshelf when I walked in, and she got awfully flustered in her rush to keep me from seeing whatever it was. I'm telling you, Clint, it's got to be important if she didn't tell me anything. Either that or . . ." Her eyes lowered and a sadness settled over her like a dark cloud. "Either that, or we're not as close friends as I thought."

Clint pat her hand consolingly and said, "I'm sure that's not the case. I know Jen well enough to say that she would never use someone like you who's just looking out for her best interests."

"I hope you're right. Really, I do."

"Of course I am. And I think you know what I said is true."

She nodded again. Her face had brightened somewhat and she no longer looked so despondent. Whenever someone moved close to her, however, she still looked at them suspiciously from the corner of her eye. When the piano player sat down in front of his instrument and the curtains started opening on the stage, she grew even more uncomfortable.

Getting up from his seat, Clint walked around and pulled out Shannon's chair. "Come on," he said. "Let's get out of here before Jen sends out a search party. I'm starving."

He led her outside and started walking toward the house. The sky was completely dark and the street was dimly illuminated by a few scattered oil lamps. When Clint turned to see how Shannon was doing, he felt her press against him as she wrapped her arms around his neck and gave him a long kiss on the mouth.

"Not that I'm complaining," he said once she pulled away. "But what was that for?"

"Just for taking the time to listen. And for coming all this way."

"You know, I killed a man to protect you."

"Then I'll have to give you the rest of my thanks a little later." Taking Clint's arm, Shannon started walking and pulled him toward Jen's house.

SEVENTEEN

Shannon Carsey and the newcomer got up and made their way out of the saloon. Shannon said a couple things to the folks who told her good night and the man tipped his hat as well, but they both seemed a little nervous. Actually, the man seemed a little nervous and Shannon seemed *very* nervous.

It took a while for them to make their way through the crowd packing into the place for the show, but they both got to the front door before too long and stepped outside. In their wake, several locals talked about them before moving on to better things. Soon, the curtains on the stage parted and a group of young dancers pranced into view to reclaim all of the attention.

All of the attention, that is, except for one man's. Although that man stood at the bar with his head cocked in such a way that made it difficult to tell exactly where he was looking, he most definitely was not looking at the stage. His eyes were narrow and obscured by hooded lids and dark bags underneath. The hat he wore looked one size too big for his head and it leaned forward over his brow like a scarecrow's. None of the others paid him too much mind, however, no matter how odd he looked. They knew him well enough to allow him to blend into the scenery. After all, with the dancers kicking up their skirts to a lively tune, there were much better things to watch than some raggedy old man.

Ben Gibsom had been sitting in that saloon for the better part of the day. There was nothing too strange about that. Short in stature, Ben looked like the life energy had somehow been drained out of him in a way that caused his color to fade and his flesh to wrap tightly around his bones as if it was hanging on for dear life.

Ben's long, gray hair made him look older than his forty-eight years. It was a life of hard work and no rewards, which made Ben feel older than his own granddaddy. A life with no loved ones and no prospects made him stop caring if his chin whiskers grew to unsightly lengths or if his hair resembled a tangled mop hanging down from his hat.

These things were old news to Ben Gibsom, but that didn't mean that he no longer thought about them. Everyone else in town considered him to be a harmless nobody who was content to live out his days in a nowhere town like Byrne, Kansas.

But that couldn't have been farther from the truth.

Ben Gibsom might not have had many prospects, but that just meant that he knew to take full advantage of the ones that presented themselves. Owen Prowler had presented such a prospect and it was a rich one, indeed.

All a man had to do was keep his eyes and ears open for any information that a man like Prowler would need. It could involve a wanted man passing through town, a railroad employee looking to expand, or some folks in town up to no good. Once he'd gotten to have a talk with Mr. Prowler, Ben found out that the man was interested in other types of information as well. Such things as a lawman with a smudge on his record, a politician with gambling debts, or some newspaper reporter who knew a little more than he should. All of that could be worth a pretty penny, even if it wasn't involving people from the town of Byrne.

Even a new arrival in town was information that could be worth a couple dollars. Especially if that arrival was involved with a woman who'd caught Mr. Prowler's interest as of late. The price for information involving such a man could only jump once that same man gunned down one of Prowler's own workers.

And if Prowler knew that that same man was none other than The Gunsmith, himself . . . well . . . even a man as miserable as Ben Gibsom had to smile at that prospect.

Sure, Ben knew who that man with Shannon Carsey was. He'd seen Clint Adams the last time he was in Byrne. One of the advantages of having no family or steady work was that it gave a man plenty of time to sit around and watch what went on. And one of the advantages of watching what went on in Byrne was that there was a man who was always willing to pay to know what was seen.

Ben thought about all of this as Shannon Carsey and Clint Adams made their way out of the Sundowner. After enough time had gone by and most everyone inside was occupied with the dancing girls, Ben started heading toward the door himself. As usual, nobody really took any notice of him except for shifting in their seats to look around him if he blocked their view of the stage.

That was all well and good. Ben had learned to take advantage of being ignored. After all, it did have certain advantages. Especially when he was trying to get even more information so he could sweeten the pot when he went to barter with Prowler.

So far, Ben had plenty to give. But if he could get a little more, it could only mean more money for himself. When he got out of the saloon, he had to stop himself short. As soon as he'd gone through the door, he'd almost immediately stumbled upon the two people he was trying to follow.

If he didn't know any better, Ben would have sworn that he'd caught the tail end of a kiss between those two. They were looking at each other with enough heat for even a withered old man to feel. In fact, Ben knew they were kissing, because when they turned to walk away, they did so arm in arm, without even noticing that he'd nearly walked right into them.

Ben didn't have to follow them all the way for him to know where they were headed. It was obvious that they were going back to the Dawson widow's place, and they seemed to be in a mighty hurry as well. Before he broke away from them to head to his own modest home on the other side of town, Ben noted just how close the pair seemed to be.

A lot of the feeling he got was on Shannon's part, but he didn't really expect a man like Clint Adams to be fawning over a woman. Besides, what he'd seen was plenty of what he was looking for.

Those two were sweet on each other. Shannon was sweet on him, that was for sure. At the very least, Adams cared about her and that was something Prowler would most definitely be interested in knowing. Ben was sure of that.

EIGHTEEN

Jen's house was filled with the smells of dinner. If Clint had been starving before, his stomach felt like a bottomless pit once the food started getting piled up onto his plate. There was the roast she'd promised, as well as mashed potatoes, green beans and corn on the cob. She even brought out a loaf of white bread which all began to fill the grumbling hole inside of him.

As they all dug into their meals, conversation turned to more mundane topics such as local gossip and events that had occurred in Clint and Jen's lives in the years since they'd seen each other. For the most part, nobody brought up Robert except in passing. Clint avoided the topic to keep from darkening the pleasant atmosphere in the little dining room, and Jen seemed happier to focus on happier times.

By the time she'd cleared the table and returned with coffee and the pie she'd made, Jen seemed almost back to the way Clint remembered her: cheerful and full of life. The pie was so good that Clint practically disappeared from the conversation altogether. But Shannon was there to take up the slack, and she started in on some chatter about a mutual friend of theirs whom Clint had never heard of.

Finally, they all reached the point where their stomachs were full and they had to drop their forks. Clint leaned back in his chair and wiped his mouth with the linen napkin that Jen had insisted be on his lap at all times.

"Good lord above," Clint said. "That was one hell of a meal."

Jen smiled and got up to clear away the plates. "You sure you don't want another piece of pie? I'd hate to see the rest of it go to waste."

"If I had one more bite, I think I'd burst. Why don't you let me help with the cleanup?"

"Heavens no. Just sit and drink your coffee. You're a guest in my home and I won't have you cleaning up. It's just a pity that you won't allow me to serve up another slice—"

"Please . . . don't even say it," Clint groaned. "If you think I won't finish off that pie while I'm in town, then you need your head examined."

Jen smiled at him in a way that beamed like pure sunshine. Right before she looked away, however, Clint detected something else in her eyes that didn't match the happiness on her face. She turned away quickly, worried perhaps that Clint had seen what she'd been trying so hard to hold back.

"You all right?" he asked her.

The widow tried to put on a casual smile, but fell just short of success. She nodded weakly and went about the task of running her plates from the dining room into the kitchen. "I'm all right. Just a little tired, is all."

Clint knew better than to offer to help again, since Jen seemed so fixed on completing her simple chores. When she was done, she leaned on the back of a chair as though she needed it to support her weight. Her face was flushed and she was more than a little pale.

"Actually . . . I'm very tired."

Clint got up to stand beside her. Reaching out for Jen's arm, he said, "You look like you're about to fall over. Can I get you anything?"

"No, I just need some rest."

"Then why don't you get to bed? I can let myself out."

Looking a little disappointed, she said, "But I thought you'd stay here. I wouldn't want you to have to pay for a room after coming all the way from New York. Especially after what happened at the station."

"You've got enough on your plate without having to worry about me," Clint said soothingly. "Now, I'm going to help you upstairs and then I can get out of here to leave you be. I'll hear no more of it."

She started to resist, but finally nodded and began walking toward the narrow staircase leading to her upper floor. Although she didn't seem to have any trouble walking, Jen still held onto Clint's hand the entire way. Her steps were slow but sure and she leaned on the banister more than the arm that Clint offered.

At the door to her room, Jen straightened up and turned to look at him. "You're a godsend, Clint. Maybe I can be more of a help in all of this tomorrow when I have some more wind in my sails. Right now, I need to sleep."

"Then go on and get your sleep, Jen. I'll come by tomorrow and we can see about clearing up this mess of yours."

"If you like, I'm sure Shannon will keep you company for a while. She might be able to answer some questions or fill you in on a few things. I just don't have the energy to go through it all again right now. I wish—"

Clint silenced her by putting a finger over her lips and then kissing her on the cheek. "I'll see you tomorrow. Go get some sleep."

That was all he needed to say. Jen nodded with gratification and turned to head into her room. She pushed the door shut behind her, but it only bounced off the jamb before swinging open a few inches. Clint stayed out in the hall to make sure that she was doing all right. When he saw her lay down on the bed without changing into a nightgown or even pulling back the covers, he figured she would be fine and walked quietly down the stairs.

When he stepped back into the small living room, Clint found Shannon standing at the window, peering through the thin curtains with her arms folded over her chest. Her head turned at the sound of his footsteps, but she looked back outside once Clint moved in to stand behind her.

"She's like that a lot ever since Bobby was killed," Shannon told him. "She seems to be fine and then she doesn't even have the strength to keep on her feet."

"That's to be expected. She's been through a lot."

There was a few moments of silence before Shannon looked over her shoulder toward the stairs. "Is she asleep?" she asked in a hushed voice that reminded Clint of their stifled conversation in the saloon.

"I'm pretty sure she was out before I made it back down the stairs."

"Then maybe this is a good time to show you what I was talking about before."

Clint felt a little strange about sneaking around in Jen's own home, but he figured that might be the only way for him to see what was going on. After all, he couldn't do much to help if he just talked about local gossip and half-formed suspicions.

"All right," he said. "Let's see what you were talking about."

NINETEEN

To anyone who was new in town, it might have seemed a little strange that the newspaper offices were open at such odd hours. Actually, judging by the size of Byrne itself, it might seem stranger that the town had a newspaper at all. Beyond that, the newspaper seemed to be quite large. At least, that was judging by its offices.

To anyone who was new in town, it might have seemed very odd indeed that there would be armed men posted outside the offices. While the *Byrne City Examiner* seemed prosperous enough, surely there wasn't a need to guard a press and a few desks. But there was no mistaking the fact that those two men standing in the *Examiner*'s doorway were guards.

Both men were armed and sporting their weapons for all to see. Also, they didn't even have the inclination to talk to one another during the quiet hours of their duty. Instead, they just stood there and glared into the growing darkness like imposing statues. The only time they'd moved was to hold open the door next to their post as two men shuffled inside dragging a heavy load of blood-soaked canvas between them.

The door that the guards held open was to another business that just happened to be open at that late hour. Unlike the *Examiner,* however, that other business was only open late because of special circumstances. After all, it wasn't every day that one of Owen Prowler's men was gunned down in his own town.

The undertaker's parlor had a single light inside, which stayed on long after the two men had left, after delivering the body of the kid in the vest. Once those two left, the guards kept right on watching as the sheriff led them off to spend the night in the jail.

"Come on, Mr. Prowler," one of the farmhands had said up to the window where they knew the man would be watching. "You ain't gonna let us go to jail, are you?"

Like a ghost appearing from a shadow, Prowler's face had appeared in a window of the second floor of the newspaper office. The man was dressed in black, which made his face not only look paler than normal, but also as though it floated disembodied behind the glass.

Prowler's only reply to the farmhand's plea was a stony glare directed into the young man's eyes. His glance shifted over to the lawman, followed by a stern nod of his head before Prowler disappeared once again into the shadows.

"You saw the man," Sheriff Larkins said. "Looks like you'll be bunking down in a cage tonight."

Once the lawman had dragged the two kids down the street to his office, the pair of guards remained quiet and still at their posts. Every so often, a flicker from the lantern inside the undertaker's place made it look as though one of the men had twitched, but that was just a trick of the light. As the night went on, the men stayed planted in their spots.

Neither of them moved a muscle until they spotted a hunched-over figure approaching the newspaper office from the other end of the street. They recognized him immediately, nodding to him as he shuffled up to the *Examiner*'s front door.

Owen Prowler worked in a room all by himself in the office that used to belong to the *Examiner*'s editor before Prowler had bought out the paper entirely. Now the editor was set up in one of the smaller rooms down the hall, and Prowler situated himself in the expansive space that took up most of the newspaper's second floor.

For a room that was practically his home, it was sparsely furnished. Most of its space was filled with shelves of ledgers and locked strongboxes which housed the information that he held so dear. Even if someone could make it past the guards outside the building, they wouldn't be able to make out a single word of any of the ledgers' coded entries.

But such a man would have had to make it past Prowler himself, as well as the silver-plated .38 pistol that hung from a holster beneath his left arm. Anyone who knew a thing about Prowler knew that the pistol wasn't just there for show. It could appear in his hand quicker than his scowl could appear on his face, and it rarely had to speak once before winning whatever argument it was in.

The office was almost completely dark. Only one solitary candle was lit, and that sat on a table in the corner next to his desk. Its weak, flickering light was barely enough to touch every one of the room's four walls, but it was all that Prowler required. He sat at his desk with his back bolt-straight and the pen in his hand working feverishly over his most recent ledger.

His steely gray eyes hardly even scanned what he was doing as he scribbled in code and checked various boxes along the side of his blotter. He didn't have to see what he was doing. It was his business to remember every last thing about it, and that included exactly what he needed to write and exactly where he needed to write it.

When he walked about his office, he sometimes did it with his eyes shut. The stern lids closed, making his clean-shaven face seem featureless as it blended up to his smooth, bald head. The creases in his flesh were deep and jagged, as if they'd been etched by time with a dull fork. His body was lean and covered in expensive suits usually made from dark-colored silk.

The sound of his pen scratching along the inside of his ledger filled the room like an insect's legs scraping along the floor. That, mixed with the shallow rustle of Prowler's breathing, were the only signs of life inside the room. The man himself had his eyes closed and hadn't moved in some time.

A tapping drifted up from the lower floor. The sound barely made it up to Prowler's office, but it had reached his ears and caused him to immediately stop what he was doing. When the tapping came again, Prowler's eyes shot open and he set the pen down as though he was going to jab it into the top of his desk.

He got up from his chair and went to the top of the stairs, his feet making no more than an occasional pat against the boards. "What is it?" he said to the men below in a voice that carried like a falcon's screech.

The front door opened and one of the guards spoke. "Someone here to see you, Mr. Prowler."

"I'm busy. Tell him to come back tomorrow during business hours."

The guard was reluctant, but spoke up without too much delay. Too much delay was the best route to Prowler's bad side. "He says he's got some information."

"It's too late, dammit! I'm not in the mood to listen to some local peddling gossip."

"He says it's about what happened at the train depot."

That was enough to make Prowler suck in a deep breath and make the walk all the way down the stairs. He moved pass the dormant printing press like a wraith floating between tombstones; his head held low and his shoulders pinched forward. Except from the smooth motion of his legs, he seemed utterly motionless. His eyes were fixed on the door in front of him as well as the guard's face peeking inside.

Anticipating the next question, the guard said, "It's Ben Gibsom, the old man who—"

"I know who he is," Prowler snapped. Moving to the edge of the doorway, he peered out into the night at the frail-looking figure waiting there amid the two armed men. "What do you want, Ben? It's late."

"I know who shot your boys today."

"So do I. He's keeping company with the Dawson widow and put up a fine looking horse in the livery. You got anything else for me?"

"How about his name?"

Prowler studied Ben for a total of half a second. After that, he stepped to one side and started walking back toward the stairs. "Come in, Ben. Talk to me."

TWENTY

Clint followed Shannon through Jen's house. She led him away from the window and toward a narrow doorway that was between the living room and the dining room. If the door had been closed, it might have been mistaken for a closet, but that wasn't too surprising considering the scale of everything else inside the house.

The home was compact and yet quaint. There were enough niceties laying about that Clint felt as though he might knock something over at every turn. Between the end tables, mirrored wall hangings and little cabinets everywhere, there was hardly enough space for a man to get around comfortably.

That sense of nervous claustrophobia didn't get any better once Clint stepped into the room where Shannon led him. In fact, it got a little worse. Here, there was a fireplace along one wall and several bookshelves set up around all the others. Clint had seen the room in passing once before, but hadn't actually gone inside until now. He had to lower his head a bit to get through the doorway, but he felt his senses open up once he'd gone through.

Shannon was already standing at one of the shelves, reaching out but not touching a row of books. "This is where I saw her those times I was telling you about. She was looking at something right around here, and I think she hid it on this shelf."

Clint walked up to her and took a look of his own. "Well, I'm not about to go rooting through her things, if that's why you brought me here."

"No, not at all. I just thought that there might be something here you recognize. Maybe you see something that meant something to Bobby or . . ." Her voice trailed off and she stepped away from the shelf. "I don't know what I expect, really. Just looking to see if there's a needle in the haystack."

Although Clint still wasn't entirely comfortable with the notion of sneaking around while Jen slept upstairs, he decided it wouldn't do any harm if he just glanced over the things that were in plain sight. After all, if he spotted anything that way, then that meant Jen had probably wanted it to be found.

That line of reasoning wasn't the best, but it suited Clint for the time being.

Keeping his hands to his sides, Clint leaned toward the shelf and perused its contents as if he was in a museum. At first, he hurried his eyes along, still feeling somewhat guilty for being in that room at all. The shelves contained a mixture of books, papers and other little trinkets that didn't have a rightful place anywhere else in the house. Some of those included a frog made out of clay and painted green, as well as a brass container made for storing matches, with a woman's cameo engraved on its lid.

Once he looked past those things, Clint concentrated more on what could actually have some meaning regarding the current situation. As far as that went, Jen could have been hiding any of the papers or documents that were stuffed in between the books. When Clint thought about rifling through those, he felt a pang of guilt similar to what he'd felt only a few moments ago.

Shannon seemed to sense that and came up beside him. "Whatever she was hiding, it was more in this area," she said, while pointing toward the end of the shelf more populated by books and papers than knickknacks.

Clint was just about to abandon his halfhearted search when something caught his eye. "What's this?" he said more to himself than to the woman beside him.

Leaning in a little closer, Shannon asked, "What's what?"

His eyes focused on something wedged in between a pair of books with nothing written on the bindings, Clint moved his hand toward the flat piece of paper that seemed to be wrapped with dull, coppery thread. It didn't look like thread, however. And it didn't look like copper. Whatever it was caught the light and gave off just a bit of reflection . . . just enough to catch Clint's eye.

The piece of paper was no wider than a bookmark, which was exactly what Clint had thought it was. He'd thought that right until that strange thread caught his eye. Since he was looking for anything that seemed unusual, he decided to pull the paper out and have a quick look at it for himself.

It slid out from between the books and came free a little sooner than he'd been expecting, since it turned out to be a little shorter than a bookmark. The thread was wrapped all the way around the bottom half of it and tied off with a piece of thin, black ribbon.

The paper was cut into the shape of a hand with fingers extended. Along the base of the palm was written a date and a line from the scripture, expressing "good thoughts for the dearly departed." Seeing that, Clint realized that it wasn't thread wrapped around the cutout, but several strands of hair.

Since the date was a few weeks ago, he could only assume that it was Bobby's hair.

TWENTY-ONE

"That's the funeral notice," Shannon said matter-of-factly. "The family members each got one."

Although Clint had seen such things before, he still reflexively moved his thumb away from where it had been resting on top of the strands of tightly wrapped hair. Bobby had been somewhat of a friend, but thinking that the rest of that hair was sticking out of a decaying scalp sent a chill down Clint's spine.

He handed the card over to Shannon as if for her to inspect it, but he was more than happy to get it out of his grasp. That was when his eyes fell upon another small item sitting on the end of the shelf. Reluctantly, his hand went to it, but he didn't pick it up.

"Do I even have to guess what that is?" he asked while nudging a small, braided broach that appeared to have been woven out of the same thread.

Shannon took a look and reached out to take it. Running the broach through her fingers, she smiled warmly. "That's made out of Bobby's hair as well. The undertaker's wife makes these special for widows and children sometimes. Isn't it lovely?"

"Sure it is." Clint let his comments end there, moving

his finger along the line of books and stopping at the spot where the funeral notice had been found. "What's this?" he asked quietly, while pulling out a book that was noticeably smaller than the others.

It was a black, leather-bound volume that was about the same size as a deck of playing cards. On its cover were letters engraved in gold, written in flowing, ornate script. The spine was engraved with words that Clint thought might have been Latin. On the cover was the phrase "For your time of loss."

Clint opened the small book to its first page. The paper inside was thin and delicate, reminding him more of tissue than anything that could stand the imprint of pen or press. The script was similar to that on the cover; fine and ornate. He only needed to read a couple lines before he recognized the words as quotes from the Good Book itself.

"This has the same date as the one written on the notice," Clint pointed out.

Shannon took one quick look, nodded, and glanced back to the broach in her hand. "That's her mourner's Bible."

Just then, Clint was realizing how long it had had been since he'd been through all the motions of a proper burial. He was no stranger to death, that was certain, but funerals and such were a whole other side of that coin than the one he was used to.

He'd been to plenty of funerals in his time and could remember quite a few that stuck out in his mind, but there were plenty of rites and rituals that went along with them that Clint usually didn't take part in. For example, he'd heard about the braids and decorations made from the deceased's hair such as the broach that Shannon was admiring. Some people even made miniature dolls out of such hair collected from the dead. Clint had seen one of those some time ago, which looked similar to the stick figure that a child would have drawn in the sand.

At some of the funerals he'd attended, Clint had seen several different types of things presented to the family or widow. At the time, he'd merely paid his respects and left them to their weeping. It had never occurred to Clint to walk up and ask the bereaved what it was they were holding.

He still held the small book in his hand, feeling the pages crinkle beneath his fingers as he slowly turned them over. "This doesn't look like a Bible I've seen before. I mean . . . I recognize some of the passages, but they don't seem to be in the proper order."

"Oh it's not an entire Bible. It's a bunch of selections that are for someone to read who's grieving for a loved one. It's supposed to give them comfort . . . just like the cover says."

Clint flipped through the little book, scanning the selected passages and noting where some of the pages were folded down on the upper corner. The paper was still a clean white, making the book seem all the more delicate and new. He came to one section that stayed open more than the rest of the book. It was a passage that told of how the departed soul would find comfort in the arms of their lord.

The page wasn't folded down, but the book seemed to want to stay open to that page, as if it had been held in that spot for more time than any other. Clint noticed a smudge on the bottom corner, and when he looked a little closer, he saw it was a small, circular water stain that had distorted some of the words.

Seeing that smudge, he got a clear picture of Jen looking down at that same page, reading the words over and over again as her tears fell down from her cheeks. In fact, Clint could almost feel the wetness on his finger from the tear that had stained the very page he was reading.

With that picture clearly in mind, he lost what little

desire he'd had to continue rummaging through the widow's personal things.

"Let's get out of here," he said. "If there's something Jen wants us to know, then she'll tell us. As far as her hiding anything, I think she may just not be comfortable grieving in front of an audience."

Shannon's face reflected some determination and it looked as though she was about to insist on continuing their search. She looked at the Bible as well, however, and squinted her eyes. "Can I see that?" she asked.

Clint handed her the book and watched as she looked down at the same, tear-stained page. Letting out a slow breath, Shannon nodded and looked up from the Bible.

"You're right, Clint. We don't have any business doing this." Holding the open Bible in the palms of her hand, she asked, "You don't think I'm a bad person, do you?"

"Of course not. You're just concerned. Times like these are hard for everyone, and with all that's happening with this Prowler person, I don't blame you at all for being on edge."

Shannon nodded and looked down once again at the Bible. As she did, the pages rustled as if a disturbance in the air had set the flimsy paper into motion. For a moment, it seemed as though a ghostly hand was turning them to look at another selection of passages. When the pages stopped, they were open to one of the passages marked by a folded corner.

Glancing down reflexively at the book, Shannon and Clint both tried to get a look at the newly revealed pages. Neither of them read the words right away, as a sudden chill ran down both of their spines.

"Did you see that?" Shannon asked.

Clint looked up at her and then back down to the Bible. "Those pages are so thin, anything could cause them to rustle like that." To distract himself from the cold feeling that still gripped his bones, Clint started to read the words on the open pages.

Like the ones on the Bible's spine, those words appeared to be written in another language. "Can you read that?" he asked.

Shannon squinted and shook her head. "No. I've never seen writing like that."

"It's probably Latin."

"You read Latin?"

As much as he wanted to maintain the impressed look on Shannon's face, Clint couldn't bring himself to lie. "No. Just taking a guess." Taking the book from Shannon's hand, he held it and examined the spine a little closer. Looking at it from the inside, he could see a crease in the binding which wasn't yet deep enough to show through on the outside.

"It could be Greek," Clint said as he scanned the word and paragraphs again. "Whatever it is, it looks like someone knows how to read it since this page seems almost as worn as the other one."

Shannon reached out a finger and touched the tip to the corner of the page. "Plus, it's folded at the top," she said, while pulling her hand back as if she thought the paper might sting her. "Priests know how to read Latin."

"Well . . . if having a priest thumb through a Bible and read from it is cause for suspicion, then we're going to have to investigate every building with a cross on the roof. For now, why don't we just put this back and give Jen her peace."

Saying that, Clint turned to look over his shoulder. He couldn't help but feel as though he was robbing the place and the owner was going to catch him at any moment. He gently closed the book and carefully slid it back into its proper place upon the shelf.

Shannon must have been feeling the same way, because she walked with Clint and didn't say a word until they were out of the house and the door was tightly closed behind them. The night air was lukewarm and a gentle breeze was blowing through town. Lifting her face to the wind, she took in a deep breath. When she looked back at Clint, she was smiling.

"You know where the hotel is?" she asked.

"With only two main streets to choose from, I think I should be able to find it." Noticing a subtle shift in the woman's expression, Clint added, "But it's never a good move to turn your back on a willing guide." He offered his arm to her and she took it gratefully, and they both headed toward Ridgemont Avenue.

TWENTY-TWO

As Prowler climbed the stairs to his office, he reached out and twisted the knobs on the few lanterns he passed. He did so strictly out of habit rather than courtesy, since he'd long ago gotten fed up with the whining that visitors did about the lack of light. When he got to his own sanctum, however, he only turned up the light enough for his un-invited guest to see where he was going. The shadows were still the ruling faction within the dreary space.

"So what brings you here at this hour, Ben?" Prowler asked. "What news have you got for me that's so important?"

The old man didn't fidget in front of Prowler like so many others did when they were in that same room. Instead, he took a seat in the single, straight-backed chair in front of the desk and spoke in an even tone. "I know you like to hear about what's going on in this town. And after the dustup that happened at the train station, I thought you'd be especially anxious to hear about anything regarding that."

Prowler opened a carved wooden cigar box at the front of his desk. It was the only thing on the desk that could be considered even slightly decorative, despite its simple finish and the block-letter monogram set into the lid. After taking a cigar out for himself, he offered one to Ben, who accepted gratefully.

When he bit the end off the cigar, Prowler bared his teeth for a fraction of a second, giving him a brief yet savage scowl. He struck a match, which set a glow onto his stark, clean-shaven skull, which lasted right until he snuffed the flame out with a quick exhale.

"What happened at the depot was brutal violence," Prowler said after sucking in a mouthful of smoke. "Why do you think I would have anything to do with that?"

"I didn't say that at all. All I said was that you'd want to hear about it. There's still a payment coming for good information, isn't there?"

Prowler's eyes fixed on the old man for a bit, until he started to nod. "There's still a payment coming. That depends on what you have to say, though. You mentioned something about knowing the man's name who came here and killed that young man."

"I know his name all right. I recognized his face since he'd been here some time ago to—" Cutting himself off, Ben clamped his jaw around the cigar he'd been chomping on even though it had yet to be lit. He ran a hand over the bristly stubble on his chin and then wiped the sweat onto his grimy pants. "How much of a payment is there?" he finally managed to ask.

Prowler's first reaction was to glare at the old man with enough intensity that it seemed to make the burning embers of his cigar flare a little brighter. But the moment passed, and his hand never drifted any closer to the pistol beneath his arm. "You're a good man, Ben. I admire someone with a spine. And since your information has proven fruitful before, I'll set the payment at ten dollars."

"And what if it's better than that?"

"Well, then I'll just have to double it."

The old man's sunken face twisted into a fleeting resemblance of a smile as he mentally spent all that money. "The one who shot your . . . uh . . . who shot that young man was here before. He visited Robert Dawson a few years back."

"I could have pieced that together myself, since Dawson's widow was there to meet him. You'll have to impress me with something better than that or the payment goes down to zero."

"He helped Dawson when he was here. It was a matter concerning some fair amount of trouble where some other men were hurt. They was going to kill Dawson, but this other one stepped in and cleared the whole mess up."

"Yeah?" Prowler said as he puffed on the cigar. "I'm still waiting."

Ben shifted his own cigar to the corner of his mouth as he leaned forward to place the palms of his hands flat upon Prowler's desk. "The man's name is Clint Adams."

The chair squeaked beneath Prowler's weight as he leaned back and rolled the cigar between his thumb and forefinger. His eyes were still trained on the man in front of him, but he really didn't seem to be interested in Ben at all. He seemed to be staring off at something only he could see as he nodded almost imperceptibly.

"You're talking about *the* Clint Adams," Prowler said without much question.

Ben nodded quickly. "Yessir, I am."

"And do you know where he is right now?"

"He was with Shannon Carsey in the Sundowner and they were both headed back to the Dawson place from there."

Fishing a folded wad of money from his pocket, Prowler removed a pair of ten-dollar bills from beneath a simple steel clip and set it on the desk in front of Ben. "Take that and get out," he told the old man. "And if I were you, I'd find someplace real safe to go with it. The streets might not be too safe for a while."

TWENTY-THREE

The rough, uneven path that led from the small residential area to the train depot didn't even have an official name. It would have been the third real street in Byrne, but since it wasn't much more than a rutted walkway running parallel to the railroad tracks, the locals simply called it Track Walk.

It led from the cluster of homes, past some storage sheds and to the depot. Clint and Shannon walked that way at a leisurely pace, taking in the night air as they made their way to the hotel, which was next to the Sundowner. Once they were out of Jen's house and in the open, both of their moods took a dramatic upward turn.

As they walked along the tracks, neither one of them had to think about death or mourning. They didn't have to step lightly to avoid waking Jen as they snuck around below the sleeping widow. All they had to think about was each other and the path directly in front of them. In fact, as they got closer to the depot, they slowed their steps just a bit to keep from reaching the end of their walk too soon.

"Has the hotel gotten any better since the last time I was here?" Clint asked.

Shannon shrugged. "They put on a new coat of paint last week, but I'd say that's about it. I really wouldn't know, since I don't stay there myself."

"Well, after the day I've had, all I need is a bed under me and some hot coffee in the morning to make me happy."

"So you plan on staying at the hotel, then?"

Clint stopped his ambling stroll at the end of the board-walk of Ridgemont Avenue. The familiar street was to his back as he turned to face Shannon. "That's right. I don't think I would feel right imposing on Jen for a room. It just wouldn't feel right after . . ."

He was going to say it wouldn't feel right after sneak-ing through her personal belongings and rifling through the very book intended to give her spiritual comfort. But rather than bring all that up after their pleasant walk, he settled on "After all that's happened."

Holding both of his hands in hers, Shannon ran her fingers over Clint's skin and shifted on her feet. "Actually, I wasn't thinking about you staying over there."

"Really? You had a better idea?"

The nervousness was back in Shannon's face, but this time it was much different than it had been in the saloon. Now, rather than being uncomfortable and frightened, she seemed more excited, with just a bit of hesitation thrown into the mix.

"Rather than have you pay for a room at the hotel," she said, "and seeing as how you did travel all this way as a favor to Jen and me . . . I thought I could offer you a bed in my house." Her eyes darted up and down, moving be-tween Clint's face and her own feet. "That is, if you wouldn't find that too inappropriate."

For a second, Clint just watched her. The way she turned her head slightly down made her thick brown hair tumble in front of her face. He could see her chest rising and falling with a slightly quicker rhythm, and the more he watched her, the more flushed her cheeks became.

Finally, he let her off the hook by saying, "I would appreciate that, Shannon."

"Really?"

He nodded. And when he still felt some apprehension coming from her, he leaned forward to press his lips against hers. The first kiss was short, but a bit steamier than the one they'd shared earlier that evening. This time, there was no awkwardness as she moved into him just enough to get a better feel for the touch of his skin upon hers.

After the kiss, they both stood in place for a second, still looking into each other's eyes, with less than a fraction of an inch separating their mouths. Shannon was the one to lean in the second time, opening her lips as soon as she touched Clint's mouth, allowing the tip of her tongue to flick out and get a taste of him.

Feeling that little bit of warm wetness, Clint held her face with both hands and allowed himself to give her the kiss that he'd been thinking about every time he'd been alone with her. They melted into one another, taking slow, luxurious tastes of each other as their hearts began pumping achingly in their chests.

As Clint moved back to catch his breath, Shannon sucked on his lower lip before letting it go. Her eyes took him in without trying to disguise her hunger. Her hands closed around Clint's forearms and squeezed tight in a slow, steady rhythm. When she licked her lips, she leaned her head back slightly to savor the flavor of him that remained on her skin.

"I want you to come home with me," she said. "But if you really think I'll let you sleep anywhere but in my bed, you're sorely mistaken."

"I never thought that for a second."

TWENTY-FOUR

"How far away do you live from here?" Clint asked.

She smiled warmly and opened her mouth to answer, but no words came out. Instead, her eyes suddenly grew wide and her breath caught in her throat.

Clint didn't even wonder what was wrong with her, since he'd already seen movement behind him reflected in the pupils of her eyes. The sound of footsteps thumping along the boardwalk toward him pounded in his ears like approaching thunder.

Acting purely out of reflex, Clint took hold of Shannon by the shoulders and tossed her to his left, with enough strength to get her out of the way without tossing her off her feet. She was stunned by what she'd seen, but she didn't fight him as he got her moving. In fact, she moved on her own as well and was where Clint wanted her in a matter of seconds.

With Shannon out of harm's way for the moment, Clint spun around to get a look at who was charging toward them like bulls with their tails on fire. He could see a pair of men right off the bat. They were both running down the boardwalk with grim expressions set onto their faces. One of the men had the solid build of a grizzly bear and

was brandishing a thick club in both hands. Behind that
one was a younger man who was already pulling the gun
from a holster at his side.

For a moment, Clint thought the younger man might
have been one of the men that had attacked him earlier at
the train depot. But although the youthful faces were similar in some respects, there was more intensity in the face
he saw now and none of the blind cockiness he'd seen
before.

Whoever was sending those boys had skipped past the
lightweights and was bringing out the more experienced
hands. They were experienced enough, in fact, to keep
good and quiet until they were almost directly on top of
the man they were after.

By the time Clint took in what was happening and who
was coming after him, it was too late to do anything but
try to cover up and keep from taking too much damage
right at the start. Taking the time to push Shannon out of
harm's way had worked in his attackers' favor and nearly
cost him all the teeth on the right side of his face.

The man with the club poured on the steam and reached
the end of the boardwalk even quicker than Clint had
guessed he would. By then, he'd swung the club over his
head in a tight circle, bringing it around in his left hand
as if to knock Clint's head clean off his shoulders with
the first blow.

Clint instinctively ducked his head while reaching up
with both hands. The club chopped through the air as its
wielder twisted at the last moment to compensate for what
Clint had done. But Clint knew better than to rely on him
ducking beneath the swing, and as the man lunged out to
land his blow, Clint grabbed hold of the guy's shirt and
held on with all of his strength.

Using the attacker's momentum to his own advantage,
Clint twisted his body while heaving with both arms,
sending the attacker into the air. The side of the club still

smacked against Clint's skull, but with less than half the force than the other man had intended. Clint absorbed the pain that rattled through his head and continued twisting his entire body and dragging the other man right along behind him.

The man with the club was lifted off the boardwalk and into the air, his body immediately turning toward the ground as Clint swung him down to the street. He landed on his shoulders and the back of his neck with a heavy thud, taking in most of the impact by tucking his chin down tightly against his chest.

All Clint had to see was the man with the club struggling to get back to his feet to know that the guy had landed intact. If he hadn't, the fall would have broken enough important bones to keep him from moving for a good, long while.

But Clint didn't allow himself to worry about the man with the club at the moment, since there was a gunman hot on that one's heels.

Spinning around on the balls of his feet, Clint kept himself as low as possible as he tried to get that gunman back in his sights. For a second, he couldn't see where that other man had gone off to. His eyes searched the boardwalk frantically as every passing instant worked on his nerves like a rake.

He knew that the gunman had been drawing already and would definitely have cleared leather by the time he spotted him. In fact, every moment that passed, Clint was simply waiting for the roar of a gunshot that would send fiery pain through some part of his body.

The gunshot came just as he'd expected it, and the slug hissed through the air like an angry hornet. For a second, Clint thought he'd been able to dodge the shot, but then he felt a burning pain tear down his left shoulder and back as the hot lead ripped a bloody trench through his flesh.

Clint straightened up and followed the sound of the shot

to fix his eyes immediately on the man who'd fired it. As soon as his eyes locked on target, Clint let his reflexes do the rest.

His hand flashed down to his modified Colt, plucked the weapon from its holster and brought it up in less time than it took him to blink. Although the pain from the wound on his back was shredding through his system, Clint pushed it aside and kept his arm steady as he squeezed his trigger.

The Colt bucked against his palm and let out a smoke-filled roar. The other gunman had been working his way around the side of the first building, but hadn't moved back far enough.

The gunman's face went from desperation to surprise as he felt Clint's round punch through his chest. Its impact hit him like a sledgehammer and knocked him back a step, until his back slammed against the side of the building.

Clint could hear the man with the club getting to his feet and regaining his balance, but knew better than to turn his back on the shooter again. He kept his eyes focused on that one since it looked as though he still had some fight left in him.

The only reason Clint didn't fire right away was that he thought the gunman might come to his senses and know that he was beaten. But that hope was dashed as the gunman raised his gun and sent another shot through the air.

Since his eyes were fixed on the gunman, Clint could tell precisely where the other man was aiming. That was the only way he was able to pull himself to one side while pulling his own trigger along the way.

Both gunshots went off simultaneously as lead crossed paths between the building and the street.

The gunman's round drilled through empty air and buried itself into a distant patch of dirt. Before he even realized that Clint had fired at the same time, the gunman felt his head snap back and fill with agony as though a railroad spike had been driven through his skull.

He bounced off the side of the building like a discarded toy and slumped to the boardwalk in an awkward heap. Blood trickled down his face, pouring from the third eye that had been blown into his forehead.

Clint spun around to deal with the man with the club. He figured that one had to be about ready to take another swing, and when he spun to get the man in his sights, Clint realized his notion had only been slightly off.

The other man wasn't about ready to swing.

He was already lashing out.

Reflexively, Clint raised his arms to cover his face from the incoming slab of wood. The club pounded into him just below his elbow, continued scraping down his arm and connected with something solid. That something was the handle of Clint's gun, and the club just managed to knock it out of his grasp.

More than that, Clint could hear more footsteps rattling over the boardwalk heading in his direction.

TWENTY-FIVE

The Colt turned once through the air and was swallowed up by the shadows. Rather than try to spot where it had landed, Clint turned to face the hulking man who swung his club as if he was trying to drive the piece of wood all the way through Clint's torso.

Clint straightened up and raised both arms over his head, making his body a slimmer target for the club to hit. Fortunately, his move had been the right one, and the club sliced through the air in front of him. The blunt end of the weapon grazed Clint's stomach and ribs, passing with enough force to cause sparks of pain inside of him with just the glancing bit of contact it got.

Waiting until the other man had fully extended his arms with his swing, Clint clasped his hands together and brought them down in a simple chopping motion. The strike caught the big man on the side of his neck, forcing him to expel a wheezing grunt.

Even with most of his blow absorbed by the thick knots of muscle in the other man's neck, Clint managed to take some of the wind from the guy's sails. In fact, he seized the opportunity he'd created for himself by lifting his arms and driving them down again into the same spot.

This time, the force of the blow caught the big man without any air in his lungs. His neck must have been hurting as well, because the second blow dropped him to one knee and almost sent him sprawling to the ground.

The big man turned to look at Clint, wearing an expression that would have been more comfortable on the face of a mountain lion. His lips were curled up with rage fueled by pain, showing a set of clenched teeth that were yellowed and crooked as tombstones.

Clint saw some movement coming from just past the big man's face and managed to twist his body just as a bulky elbow came swinging toward him. The man with the club jabbed his left elbow back and would have caught Clint in the gut if he hadn't turned at the last moment so that his back absorbed the strike instead.

Although he'd blocked the elbow, Clint still felt sharp, intense pain from it, which pulsed through his lungs and set his kidneys on fire. All of that, however, was better than getting the wind knocked out of him, since that would have given the big man all the time he needed to knock Clint's teeth through the back of his head.

Clint let the pain wash through him and used it to push him onward, knowing that the third man had already arrived and was waiting for an opening to join the fray. When he thought of that one, Clint took his eyes off of the man with the club for just a moment, so he could get a look at what else was going on around him.

Shannon was keeping well out of the club's reach while she moved around behind Clint and the man trying to knock him senseless. The third man, who'd come late to the fight, was a rail-thin specimen who was taking his time dropping down off the boardwalk and heading toward where all the action was taking place.

If Clint hadn't been specifically looking for the guy, he might have overlooked him. Not only was the third man skinny, but he was dressed in black, so he could blend easily into the shadows. Also, he moved like an eel through slimy water; quiet and deadly.

Although he couldn't be sure, Clint thought he saw a rifle clutched in that third man's hands. As much as he would have liked to confirm that suspicion, he thought it might be a good idea to get his mind back on the club-wielding lunatic in front of him before his brain was caved in by that same man.

Although he'd only looked away for a heartbeat, Clint thought he might have made a big mistake. The man with the club was already following up his elbow strike by twisting around and bringing the blunt piece of wood toward Clint's skull with every bit of his considerable muscle behind it.

Clint knew the big man wasn't going to wear out any-time soon. In fact, it looked as though he only got angrier every time the club missed its target. So rather than try to dodge another blow, Clint raised both of his arms and brought them together to block the incoming swing.

His forearms bashed against the inside of the other's club arm, with a jarring impact. Clint didn't stop the swing altogether, but he deflected enough of its power so that it didn't wind up buried in the side of his face.

Continuing with the motion he'd started, Clint kept his arms moving forward until the attacking club was pushed farther out of the way. From there, he changed direction and swung his clenched fists back toward the clubber's face.

The big man's eyes burned with fiery anger and his teeth were still clenched like an animal's. His entire body was possessed by the fury that drove his attacks, and when the last blow was diverted, his body continued to move ahead, bringing his face in closer as Clint's fists sped toward his chin.

Clint landed his double punch with so much force that it jarred him all the way down to his bones. Hitting the big man was like punching a brick wall, and the clubber hardly even moved except for his head snapping to one side.

By Clint's experience, a blow like that would have knocked most men flat onto their asses. But this time, it hardly seemed to faze his opponent. The clubber's feet were still firmly planted and his knees hadn't so much as buckled.

Click-*click*.

That sound echoed through Clint's ears like a crack of thunder. He didn't even have to see the third man to know that he was holding a Spencer rifle and had just levered a fresh round into the barrel. All that stood now between Clint and the bullet was his ability to guess where the shooter would be aiming.

Betting his life on the accuracy of his instincts, Clint waited for a fraction of a second before dropping low and bursting into motion. His initial reflex had been to roll backward and away from the clubber so he could put some distance between both incoming threats.

But rather than follow through with that, Clint was steaming forward with his head lowered and both arms open wide. He thought the shooter would probably be expecting him to move back and wasn't about to fire a round so close to his own partner.

Whichever it was, Clint's gamble had paid off. The crack of the rifle sounded through the air, and the bullet whipped several feet behind Clint a split second after he'd started in on his charge. Of course, now that he'd avoided one threat for the moment, there was still another one that had to be dealt with.

And that other threat seemed plenty angry.

Once again, Clint impacted against the clubber. Even though he caught the bigger man in the stomach, Clint still felt as though he was trying to fight a building rather than a man. His shoulder slammed against the clubber's gut, driving him a step or two backward. But rather than wait to see if he'd hurt the other man, Clint kept his head down and started pounding at the slab of muscle in front of him with both fists in quick, chopping blows.

He managed to get in three or four jabs before his ears picked up the ratcheting sound of the Spencer being re-loaded. He also heard the club slicing through the air above him. Unfortunately, it was too late for him to do much of anything about either one.

The club pounded against his shoulder blades, setting off an explosion of dull, throbbing pain. Clint could only count down the moments before the rifle sent another round speeding toward him.

TWENTY-SIX

"Out of the way, Bennie," came a voice from behind the big man with the club. "I want to put this bastard out of his misery."

The clubber, who Clint figured had to be Bennie, took hold of Clint's shoulder as though he was trying to tear a piece off for himself. He then straightened Clint up like a rag doll and grinned widely.

Clint was still reeling from the last knock he'd taken and came up just short of having enough strength to muscle away from Bennie. He pulled in a deep breath to try and clear up the fog that had started creeping in behind his eyes and brought his hands up to protect his face.

After swatting those hands aside, Bennie held his free hand up as if he was going to stab Clint in the throat. He snapped the shorter end of the club forward, sending it directly toward the spot between Clint's eyes.

Acting more out of desperation that anything else, Clint tossed his head back and to one side, allowing the club's handle to tear over his cheek and keep right on going. It didn't feel too good, but it was a hell of a lot better than the pain that would have followed if Bennie had done what he'd wanted.

When Clint was turned at that awkward angle, he could see some movement behind him. His eyes weren't focusing at their best just then, but he could still make out the color of Shannon's dress as well and the shape of her body as she crawled in the shadows near the railroad tracks.

Clint only lifted his head enough to get a look at what Bennie was doing. Even as he did that, he was already bringing up his right leg in a straight, powerful kick. When he caught sight of Bennie's face, Clint was just in time to see the big man's features twist into a mask of pain as he felt Clint's knee bury itself solidly into his lower abdomen.

This time, Bennie hadn't been ready to absorb a blow like that, and it felt to him as though Clint's leg wasn't going to stop until it bounced against his spine. The big man let out a deep, strained groan, and the hand that had been gripping Clint by the shoulder loosened enough for him to slip out.

Wrenching free of the massive paw that was Bennie's hand, Clint stepped back with one foot and sent it sailing forward half a second later. Now that he could see how the bigger man was positioned, he could aim the second kick much better than the first.

His boot tore through the air and slammed in almost the precise spot that he'd hit before. Except, this time, he pushed his foot out until he had all his momentum behind it. Once he felt the front of his boot drive deeply into Bennie's gut, Clint straightened his knee and pulled his kick up so that it hooked up underneath the big man's rib cage.

It was one of those moments in a fight that would live in the back of Clint's memory for years. He wasn't an expert in fisticuffs and he might not even be able to perform that same kick again, but even he had to admit that it was a thing of beauty. But even more impressive than that was the look that had settled onto Bennie's face.

First, his jaw dropped open as the breath came rushing out. He tried to make a noise, but simply didn't have any wind left. Next, he reached back to take another swing, but the club fell from his hands and finally he dropped to his knees. Bennie stayed right there, holding his gut for a moment before dropping over to one side.

Clint's eyes flashed over to the man with the Spencer rifle. All he saw was the barrel swinging toward him, with the shooter glaring angrily down the cold, rounded steel.

"Your gun, Clint!"

The voice was Shannon's, and when Clint spared a quick glance over his shoulder, he could tell that she had his pistol in hand and was tossing it closer to him.

Although he could hear the Colt land in the dirt, Clint figured it was still at least four or five feet behind him. He didn't waste another instant as he dropped down into a low squat and pushed himself back with both legs.

A gunshot cracked from the boardwalk as the Spencer let a piece of lead fly through the air where Clint had been standing less than a second ago. The man behind the rifle wasn't wasting time either, as he quickly worked another round into the barrel.

Clint tucked his chin down near his chest and rolled over his back, shoulders and neck before his legs came around to drop behind him. As he went, Clint felt himself rolling over something that gouged into his aching back. The pain was a godsend, however, as soon as he saw that he'd rolled over his own modified Colt.

With the sound of the Spencer being cocked and loaded once again rattling in his ears, Clint swiped his hand down and grabbed the Colt from the ground directly in front of him. The moment his eyes caught sight of the rifleman, Clint's gun spat a single round through the air.

The rifleman's finger tensed on the trigger, but was yanked from beneath the guard as his body was spun in a tight circle by the bullet which tore through his right shoulder. The Colt barked again and before any pain could register in the rifleman's mind, the second bullet punched through his skull and dropped him next to the corpse that was still slumped against the building.

Clint holstered his weapon and turned to see where Shannon had gone. "Are you all right?" he asked, thinking about the stray rifle bullets that had flown in her direction.

For a moment, there was only silence.

Slowly, Shannon started moving again. As she did, it became obvious that she'd been covering her head with both hands and was only now peeking out again. It took her a second to see that Clint was the only man left standing, and when she saw that, she jumped up to her feet.

Clint wanted to go to her, but he wasn't fast enough. Before he knew it, she had run into his arms.

"Thank the lord, you're all right," she said as she held on to him with all her strength.

"Actually," Clint said as he suppressed a pained grunt when Shannon's arms closed around his tender ribs and back, "I should be the one to thank you."

"Let's get out of here before any more of those men show up."

Clint heard a low moan from Bennie as the big man started to come around. Silencing him with a swift boot heel to his temple, Clint led Shannon away. "Yeah. Let's get out of here."

TWENTY-SEVEN

On the way back to Shannon's house, Clint noticed that there was hardly anyone arriving at the scene of the fight. Even with two dead bodies laying on the boardwalk and another man unconscious in the street, nobody deemed it necessary to do anything more than look out their windows and gape from a distance.

That told Clint a lot about the power structure of the town. No matter how small Byrne might have been, it still had a sheriff, and that sheriff should have been on his way the moment shots were fired. Apparently, this Prowler person that he'd been hearing so much about had arranged for his men to have their way without any interruptions.

Either that, or Sheriff Larkins was drunk and asleep in his office.

Honestly, Clint didn't much care which option was the truth. Regardless of the who's and why's, his bones were still aching and his body felt like it had been dragged from the back of a runaway stagecoach. He tried to keep up appearances for Shannon's sake, but by the time he got to her house, he was ready to keel over.

"Are you all right?" Shannon asked after closing her

front door and dropping the latch into place. "You look like you're about to keel over."

Clint forced a grin onto his face and said, "I'll be fine. Nothing that some bandages . . . and about a week in bed won't cure."

"Now I think you're playing it up a bit," she said while helping Clint get up the stairs to the second floor. Unlike Jen's home, Shannon's second floor consisted of a short hall with a door on either side. She kicked open the door on the left and took Clint into a comfortable bedroom.

"If you think you need to play on my sympathy, then you can save your breath." Angling Clint toward the bed, she eased him down onto the mattress and then eased herself down on top of him. "You've already impressed me, Clint Adams. And you've already shown me more excitement than I've ever known could be in this town."

Clint savored the feel of her body on top of him. Her legs were positioned on either side of his hips, allowing her to get close to him without putting too much weight on him. She leaned down so that her hands were on either side of his face, lowering her lips onto his with a soft, gentle kiss.

As her lips brushed against his, she squirmed ever so slightly. Shannon moved her hips back and forth over Clint, brushing against him just enough to let him know she was there. When she felt the hardness between his legs, she grinned and ended the kiss with a flick of her tongue.

Clint admired her deep, dark eyes for a moment, until he felt something wet drop onto the side of his face. Looking up to where the drop might have come from, he saw a dark red stain on Shannon's upper arm that was bleeding through her sleeve.

"You're bleeding," he said as he started to get up. "Did you get hit?"

At first, Shannon looked as though she didn't know

what he was talking about. Then, when she glanced down to where Clint was looking, she recoiled and straightened up.

"What's that?" she said in a voice full of surprise.

Clint moved out from under her and got off the bed. She sat on the edge of the mattress, her skin turning paler by the moment, the more she looked at her blood-soaked dress.

"It looks like it might be a bullet wound," Clint said. "But since you didn't really notice it until just now, I'd say it's probably not that bad."

"Are you a doctor? You can't even see it yet."

Clint gently pushed up the sleeve of her dress and was careful not to touch the wound. "I'm no doctor, but I have had some experience with gunshot wounds. Now, just try to take it easy or you'll make it worse." Glancing into her eyes, he added, "Or are you just trying to play on my sympathy?"

Panic had been seeping into her face, but it slowly started to fade and was eventually replaced by a weary smile. "All right, you made your point." Her face twisted a bit when Clint tried to roll her sleeve up past the point where most of the blood was coming from. "Ow. That hurt. It feels like it might be bad."

"That's just because I nicked it, that's all. I'm going to need to get a look at it before I can do much for you, though."

"Here," she said while shrugging away from his hand. Looking down at her bloodied dress, she slid her fingers beneath the upper edge of her top and moved the material over her shoulder. Shannon stopped before the top came down too far, however. "I can't get my other hand up there, Clint. Could you help me?"

Clint put his hand on top of hers and moved it slowly up along her arm. When he came to the first trace of blood, he lifted his hand up and looked at her face. All the pain was gone from her eyes. In fact, Shannon seemed just as anxious for him to put his hands on her as she was for him to take care of her wound.

"I'll try to be gentle," he said as he moved both hands to her shoulder and pulled the top away from her skin. Clint eased the shoulder of her clothing down over the wound and kept going until Shannon could slip her arm out of the sleeve.

Still holding the upper edge of her top between his fingers, Clint watched as she held her arm up and took a look at the shallow wound.

"There's a lot of blood," she said, even though it seemed that she obviously wasn't feeling a lot of pain. "What do you think?"

Clint looked down at her smooth, tanned skin. A fair amount of blood had seeped from the wound, but once he cleared some of that away with a cloth she gave him, he could see the wound for what it truly was. "It's just a scratch. A deep scratch, but nothing more besides that." Rubbing his hands up and down along her arm on either side of the wound, he added, "You got lucky."

Keeping her eyes fixed on his, Shannon smiled a bit and enjoyed the feel of Clint's hands moving along her flesh. She used her other hand to lightly caress the bruises and scrapes that were evident on Clint's face, scalp and neck. "I'm not the only one."

"Well, it's a good thing I'm staying here tonight. Because we can save a trip to the doctor if we just take care of each other."

"I like the sound of that."

TWENTY-EIGHT

Owen Prowler stood outside of the *Byrne City Examiner* office like a gargoyle haunting the top of a cathedral. His shoulders were thrust back and his head hung low, giving him a coiled, tense appearance. His cigar burned between his lips, flaring every so often as he pulled in a smoky breath before exhaling a black cloud.

The guards stood on either side of him, flanking him without saying a word. They'd been there for the last several minutes, waiting quietly as the sound of gunshots eventually rolled in from around the corner and down the street. Only one of them was the same guard that had been there when old Ben had paid his visit.

Prowler responded to the shots by nodding as if the bullets were speaking a language that he not only understood, but agreed with wholeheartedly. Every minute or two, he would flick the ashes of his cigar onto the ground before pulling in another helping of acrid smoke.

After a few rounds of shots, which sounded like firecrackers by the time they reached the *Examiner* office, the guards started shifting on their feet. As anxious as they got, they knew better than to express those feelings to their employer. Besides that, they didn't have to wait too long before a solitary figure walked up from Ridgemont Avenue, turned the corner and started heading toward the *Examiner* building.

"There he is," said the guard who'd been at his post the entire night. "I should go ask him if there's anyone followin—"

"Shut up," Prowler snapped. "Let him tell his story when he gets here."

The tension from the guard's nerves exuded from him like the pressure that rolled in before a thunderstorm. Even so, he stayed put and didn't move an inch from his post.

The figure making his way up the street was the second guard that had been standing in front of the door earlier that night. He walked at a normal pace right up to the point where he saw that Prowler was among the men waiting for him on the boardwalk.

"Did you see what happened?" Prowler asked from behind the cigar, which cast a dim red glow across his face.

Stepping up onto the boardwalk, the guard took one look behind him and turned to face his boss. "Yes, sir. I saw it."

"Don't make me draw it out of you one sentence at a time, man, just tell me what happened."

"We saw them together just like you said we would."

"Adams and Shannon Carsey?"

"Yeah. They were at the Sundowner, but had already gone back to Miss Dawson's place by the time we got there." The guard spoke in a low growl of a voice. He seemed anxious to say his piece, but not too anxious to hear how Prowler was going to react. As such, he made sure to keep his distance from the other man and that his answers were quick and to the point.

"We asked around the saloon and—"

"Who's this 'we'?" Prowler interrupted. "You mean you, that other kid, James and that gorilla Bennie?"

"Yeah."

"Go on."

"Well, all of us asked around and everyone saw Adams talking to Miss Carsey for a while, but nobody really heard what they said."

Prowler nodded to himself and pictured his men roaming through the saloon. He knew for a fact that someone else had been there to see the conversation. In fact, he was even starting to think that old Ben might have heard more than he'd let on. It wouldn't have been too unusual for someone like that to hold out for more money before telling all that he knew.

"So you went to Miss Dawson's house, I presume?"

Again, the guard was quick to respond with a nod of his head. "But we didn't just storm into the place. You told us to keep a low profile until we knew it was a good time to—"

"I know what I told you," Prowler said, cigar smoke drifting out from between clenched teeth. "Now tell me something I *don't* know."

"We didn't have to wait too long before Adams and Miss Carsey came back out again. They seemed to be pretty close and were talking about getting him checked into a hotel."

"You followed them?"

"Yes, sir. I fell in behind them and I don't think they knew I was there."

Despite the guard's size, Prowler knew for a fact that the man was a natural when it came to following people without being detected. The big man just seemed to have a knack for finding shadows that fit him just right and knowing how to take each step to keep it from being heard. Those very reasons were what made him such a valuable member of Prowler's personal entourage.

Even then, as the guard kept retelling what had happened, he spoke in a way that made everyone strain to hear it. Everyone, that is, except for Prowler himself. His ears adjusted naturally to the soft-spoken giant's tone. It was only the stupid men that couldn't adjust to their own surroundings.

"I told the others to cut around and head them off before they got to Ridgemont Avenue," the guard continued. "And then stood back and watched as the kid and Bennie moved in to take him out."

Prowler made a show of looking around at the empty street and then back to the few men in front of the *Examiner*. "And where are those three? I don't see them anywhere around here."

"The kid and James are dead. Bennie's getting fixed up at the doc's place."

The silence that followed was so thick that it nearly suffocated all three guards on the boardwalk. In that time, Prowler puffed on the cigar, rolled the smoke around over his tongue, and held it in until it started to burn his mouth. When he exhaled, it spewed out of him like steam.

"What about Adams?" Prowler asked, even though he already knew the answer.

"He got roughed up pretty good, but . . ."

"But he's still alive."

"Yes, sir. He's still alive."

"What about the woman?"

Pausing for a second, the guard asked, "Which woman?"

"*Either* one," Prowler snarled. "Last time I checked, I only needed one of those two bitches alive. It didn't matter then and it doesn't matter now. All I needed was *one* of them alive and the other one dead." When he said that last word, Prowler's entire face flared with the red glow of the cigar smoldering in his mouth.

Exhaling a thick cloud of noxious smoke, Prowler relaxed somewhat, as though he'd set some of his anger adrift with the cigar's fumes. "Did you or any of those monkeys who work for you get one of those women?"

". . . No, sir."

Without saying another word, Prowler turned and headed back into the *Examiner* office. The door bumped against the jamb, rattling the glass in its window.

All of the guards knew there was going to be hell to pay for what had happened. They didn't need to hear it from their boss's mouth. They could feel it like a growing vibration that shook the railroad tracks against the ground.

TWENTY-NINE

Shannon smiled at Clint as she adjusted her position on the bed. She was sitting on the edge of the mattress with him next to her. They both looked like they'd been through a grinder, but neither one of them wanted to let their wounds affect them too much.

Clint felt the aching in his body running from his boots all the way up to a powerful throbbing in his skull. But he knew from experience that things hurt even more if you thought about them too much, so he did his best to keep his mind focused on better things. Mainly, the best thing he could focus on at the moment was Shannon.

By the look in her eyes, she was thinking the same thing. Every so often, she would wince if she moved a certain way, but then she would look at Clint and the pain would melt away. Her wound wasn't that bad. It seemed that she was hurt more inside after seeing all the violence that had happened right in front of her.

Watching her as she tended to him, Clint recognized the faraway look that would come over her, and he could tell that she was thinking about something that disturbed her. But rather than let the shooting and blood get to her, she took a deep breath and set it aside.

There would be plenty of time for reflection later . . . for both of them.

She reached out to move her fingers through Clint's hair. Suddenly, she pulled her hand back and gasped sharply. "Oh my god," she said. "Clint, you're bleeding!"

"I'm sure I am. After the beating that guy back there handed me, I'm surprised I'm not—"

"No . . ." Shannon turned a little pale as she held her hand in front of Clint so he could see. Sure enough, there was enough blood on her fingers to drip down her palm, covering her skin with a dull crimson sheen.

Clint reached back to feel for himself. It hurt when he touched the bleeding spot, but no worse than the other pains that wracked his body at that point in time. He pressed his fingers through the wet, matted hair and found the wound itself.

"It's not that bad," Clint told her, while trying to wipe off his fingers as soon as possible.

"Not that bad? It looks terrible!"

"It's just a cut on my head. Those always bleed worse than anything else. It looks horrible, but it's nothing serious. Trust me."

Shannon all but jumped up off the bed, and went to a small table with a washbasin next to her dresser. "You say whatever you want, Clint. I'm going to clean that up before you pass out from all the blood pouring out of you." Working as fast as she could while primarily using only one arm, she soaked a small towel with water and wrung it out. After flipping the towel onto her shoulder, she picked up the washbasin with one hand and brought it closer to the bedside.

"Now, just turn around and sit still," she said.

Clint did as he was told, wincing slightly as the cool water was pressed into the deep scrape on his head. Although the cut itself wasn't too bad, the flesh and bone beneath it were tender from the impact that had broken the skin.

"Does that hurt?" Shannon asked in a worried tone.

Clint shook his head only slightly. "No. You're doing just fine. But don't think I forgot about that wound on your arm."

"I know you didn't forget." She wiped away most of the blood and got up to get some bandages from the next room. When she got back, she put a light dressing around his head and tied it off. "Do you think they'll be back?"

No matter how much she tried to hide it, Clint heard the fear in her voice as clear as day. After all that had happened and all she'd done for him, Clint decided to pay her the compliment of talking straight with her. "If this Mr. Prowler has any more men to throw our way . . . then yes, I'd say they'll be back."

"But not those two that tried to shoot at us."

"No. Those two won't ever be back again."

A silence fell between them as Shannon cleaned up some more of Clint's wounds. He could still feel a stinging from the gouge that a bullet had taken out of his back, but Clint stopped her before she could get too good a look at it.

"Let me see your arm," he said.

"No. You've got blood soaking through the back of your shirt and I want to—"

"We're taking care of each other, remember? Now it's my turn to take care of you."

Although she protested a little, Shannon allowed Clint to turn around and take hold of her arm. The bleeding had stopped for the most part, leaving a messy gash in her skin. Clint took the rag and wrung out some of his own blood in the washbasin. From there, he held her wrist in one hand and used the other to move the top of her dress away from the wound.

Her top was still partly off of her and had only been

covering her due to some creative positioning of the fabric around her arm. When Clint peeled away the material, he noticed that she didn't resist in the slightest. Shannon's head was tilted back slightly and she took a calm, easy breath.

"That's nice," she said as he dabbed the wet rag onto her wound.

"Does it hurt?"

"A little, but you have a gentle touch. It feels good when you put your hands on me."

After saying that, Shannon shrugged just enough so that the top of her dress fell down almost to her waist. She had her arms positioned to cover most of her, but Clint got a fine look at the side of her breasts. Her body was smooth and full-figured, and her skin was soft beneath his fingers.

It took all of his strength to keep his hands from wandering as he tended to her wound and cleaned it up with the rag. The blood cleared away fairly quickly, and the water from the rag trickled down her arm, causing her to tense slightly.

"That feels so good," she purred.

"Does it still hurt?"

"Only a little." Looking up at him, she added, "But I know you won't hurt me, Clint. And I don't want you to stop touching me."

He wrapped some bandages around her arm and let his hand ease down her side when he was finished. The edge of his thumb brushed against her breast, causing her nipple to harden.

Trading places yet again, she began pulling the shirt off of him. "Now it's your turn. Let me get a look at that back."

THIRTY

Shannon's hands felt warm and soothing on Clint's back. They were almost soothing enough to make him forget about the bloody trench that had been dug through his flesh by a piece of hot lead. Almost . . . but not quite.

When she took his shirt off, Shannon laid Clint down onto the bed with his chest pressed against the mattress. She then got some fresh bandages and a clean rag and started tending to the long wound, which started at his shoulder blades and moved like a straight trail halfway down his spine.

"Does this look worse than it is?" she asked while gently washing away the blood that had smeared on his skin.

"If I could see it, I'd let you know. But you're doing all right, so keep it up." In fact, Clint thought she was doing much more than all right. She'd climbed on top of him to get at the wound and was moving nice and easy as she examined him.

"Maybe you should go to a doctor," she said. "He might need to stitch this up."

"You're doing fine, Shannon. If I know one thing after all the hell I've been through, it's when I need to go to a doctor. I feel better already."

Clint could hear her laughing under her breath as she moved her hand down the length of the wound. Her other hand brushed along his side, moving over his skin as if she was just enjoying the feel of him beneath her fingers.

"I think you just don't want me to get off of you," she whispered.

"That could be. Is there anything wrong with that?'

"No. Actually, I don't want to get off of you, either."

The water ran down Clint's back in tiny rivulets, chilling his ribs as it made its way to the mattress beneath him. Already, the pain was easing off and Shannon was going back to the washbasin fewer times to wring out the rag. All of that confirmed Clint's own diagnosis that the wound wasn't going to cause him much trouble at all.

"It feels really good," he said. "But I can think of a way for it to feel a whole lot better."

"Oh really?" Shannon was pressing thick pads of bandages on his back, and her fingernails gently teased the skin around the dressing. "And what can I do to make you feel even better?"

"Just stay right where you are," Clint said as he twisted around beneath her. With a little bit of effort, he managed to flip over without tossing Shannon from where she was perched. Once he settled so that he was looking up at her, he sat up so that his back wasn't pressed against the sheets.

"There," he said while moving so that his hips were between her open legs. "Isn't that better?"

Shannon must have been satisfied with the way Clint's wound looked after she'd cleaned it, because she didn't seem to object too much to what he was doing. Instead, she smiled as her eyes moved down his bare chest, and she reached out to move her hands slowly over his body.

"Does your arm still hurt?" Clint asked.

"A little."

"Then let me get this out of the way." With that, Clint

pulled the top of her dress all the way down until it was bunched around her waist.

She shrugged her arms out of the sleeves, having fit the top over her somewhat while tending to Clint's back. This time, she didn't make an attempt to cover herself. In fact, she kept her eyes on him the entire time and seemed grateful once the restraint of her clothes had been removed.

Arching her back slightly, Shannon displayed her large breasts to him. The little round nipples grew rigid as he looked at them, and she shuddered a bit when Clint reached out to cup both breasts in his hands.

"Mmm," she purred as he rubbed her nipples with the palms of his hands. "That *is* a lot better."

She wriggled on top of him, sitting so that she was facing Clint with her legs wrapped around his hips. Tossing her hair back as he continued to massage her breasts, Shannon slid her fingers through his hair, being careful to avoid the spots she had just cleaned earlier.

They were both a little hesitant at first, running their hands over each other's body after dressing so many wounds. But the injuries were superficial, and they were each grateful to have such a pleasant distraction to keep their minds off of their aches and pains. In fact, Clint was feeling less and less of his pain as he concentrated on what Shannon's naked body felt like beneath his wandering hands.

Shannon let her own hands wander down past Clint's neck, over his arms and then down his stomach. From there, she reached down to rub between his legs, massaging the hardness that was growing there. When she did, she heard Clint pull in a breath that sounded anything but painful.

It was sheer reflex that caused Clint to lean in closer and press his lips against Shannon's. They kissed with even more intense passion than they had earlier. This time, it felt more like something that they'd both been waiting for after having to put it off for way too long.

Clint wrapped his arms around her back, holding Shannon tightly against him. She wrapped one arm around his neck and pressed the other around his shoulders. Together, they embraced so tightly that it seemed neither of them could breathe. Their mouths pressed even tighter together as their tongues massaged one another in an erotic dance. For the next minute or so, it felt as if they were breathing for each other, passing whatever they needed from themselves and giving it directly to the other in a heated embrace.

Shannon's hips ground against Clint's, rubbing along the hard column of flesh beneath his clothes. The more she moved, the more Clint wanted her. But as much as he wanted to be inside of her, he didn't want to break away from the kiss which kept getting better and better with each passing second.

Finally, their lips parted and they looked deeply into each other's eyes. Without a word, Shannon got off of him and they both tore at their clothes, ripping them off until there was nothing to get between their hungry bodies.

THIRTY-ONE

Clint watched as Shannon tossed her slip onto the floor and crawled on the bed toward him. All this time, he'd been admiring the ample curves of her breasts as well as the fine, shapely lines of her hips, but she was even more impressive without anything on at all. She moved like a cat across the bed, waiting impatiently for him to get into his previous position. Once he was sitting up again, she climbed onto his lap and wrapped her legs around his hips.

The feel of her skin gliding over his body made Clint's penis even harder than it already was. By the time she'd settled into her place, he was literally aching to be inside of her. All it took was a shift of his hips and a slight thrust for him to slide the tip of his cock into her moist vagina.

Shannon's body tensed and she arched her back as he slipped deeper into her. Using her feet at the small of his back, she pulled herself closer to him and ground herself against the entire length of his rigid shaft.

Savoring the feel of her hot wetness surrounding him, Clint pushed all the way inside of her, until his muscles were straining as well. The effort made the reward all the sweeter, however, and Shannon let out a soft, luxurious moan in response.

They sat there for a bit, moving slowly against each other, letting the passion build. Then they each started moving faster again. Clint moved his hips back and forth while Shannon rode him, matching his rhythm thrust for thrust.

Clint leaned back, supporting himself with his arms, and pumped solidly into her. She adjusted to him perfectly, arching her back and moving her hands back to rest on his legs. Her body was exquisite from that angle. Shannon's full breasts were thrust forward and bounced as her body began moving faster and faster. Her stomach tensed as he pumped between her legs, causing her fingers to grip him tighter with the pleasure that swept through her body.

When Clint gave a powerful thrust that drove his cock all the way into her, Shannon let out a breathy cry as the muscles between her legs tightened around him. Watching as Shannon handed herself over to her passion, Clint wanted to drive her even further.

He reached out and took her in his hands, guiding her as he moved out from beneath her. From there, Clint laid her down upon the bed and lowered himself on top of her. Shannon wriggled and squirmed as he did this, using both hands to touch him and urge him to get closer.

The moment that Clint brushed the tip of his penis against the moist lips between her thighs, Shannon grabbed his forearms and hooked one leg over his shoulder. She moaned loudly when he drove all the way inside of her, every inch of her body shuddering with the pleasure that she'd been waiting for.

Clint moved his hands up and down over her hips and thighs, grabbing tightly as he pounded inside of her and massaging as he eased out again. When he couldn't wait any longer, he took hold of her and started pumping into her, causing them both to groan with ecstasy every time their bodies connected.

His cheek moved against the heel that was resting on his shoulder, and he ran his fingers up along the bottom of her leg, which was lifted in the air. Soon, her other leg was perched up on his other shoulder, allowing Clint to move in and pump even harder inside her.

They moved with a raw, frenzied rhythm and their bodies were glistening with sweat. Clint could feel his passion building to its climax, so he slowed down and simply let his hands roam over Shannon's stomach and breasts.

She seemed anxious for him to continue, but then she reached up and placed her own hands on top of his, guiding his touch to exactly where she wanted it to go. First, she wanted him to keep his hands on her breasts, circling her erect nipples and tracing a line along the sides and then over her cleavage.

Closing her eyes and pressing her head back against the mattress, Shannon moved his hands lower along her abdomen and then to the fine contours of her hips. She guided one hand between her legs until his fingertips were brushing against her clitoris. With her other hand, she moved him to her inner thigh, where he started massaging and kneading the muscles there.

"Oh god, yes," she moaned as he traced little circles around the erect nub of her clit. "Just like that."

Clint could feel her getting wetter by the second and without breaking contact with her sensitive flesh, he slipped another finger along the lips of her vagina. She arched her back again and spread her legs, opening herself so he could ease two fingers just inside of her.

Shannon savored the feeling of his hands on and in her before moving back and getting up onto her knees. She looked at him with a hungry, playful grin and turned around, pressing her chest down onto the bed and lifting her round buttocks.

Admiring the shapely curves of her backside, Clint eased in behind her and ran his hands up over her hips. His rigid cock found her opening easily and he pushed all the way inside of her. When he'd buried his entire length between her legs, Clint felt her body tense and saw her fingernails digging into the mattress.

Taking hold of her hips, he began pumping in and out, driving deep inside of her with every powerful stroke. When Shannon tossed her hair back over her shoulders, Clint reached forward and entwined his fingers through the dark, silky strands. As he pumped into her, Clint pulled on her hair just enough so that Shannon's head came back and she let out a loud, passionate groan.

Her voice filled the room as Clint kept hold of her hair while resting the other hand on the small of her back. He kept thrusting between her legs until Shannon's body was taken over by a shuddering orgasm. Clint let go of her hair as she started tossing her head back and forth, lowering her face onto the bed so she could scream with ecstasy.

All the while, she kept grinding herself against him, moving along his cock to draw out the climax, which shook her entire body. Clint couldn't take too much of that before he felt his own orgasm coming, and he grabbed onto her hips for one final thrust before exploding inside of her.

Shannon crawled forward with the last bit of her strength and laid down on the bed with her head on a pillow. Clint got beside her and dropped down onto the mattress, landing with a solid thump as a jolt of pain lanced through his spine and ribs.

"Owww," he snarled while rolling onto his side. "I forgot about my back."

Shannon smiled and ran her fingers over Clint's chest. "And all this time, I was being so careful to keep you off of that spot."

"Oh well. After what you just did to me, a bullet wound is the last thing I want to be thinking about."

Shannon held up her arm and looked down at the bandages wrapped around her wound. The dressing seemed to be holding up fine, although there was the slightest tint of red beneath it. "All right, you've had your fun," she said, turning her attention back to Clint. "Roll onto your stomach and let me see that back."

Clint could tell the wound hadn't reopened or, at least, wasn't bleeding. All the same, he did as he was told and let Shannon fuss over him for a bit.

"Maybe you should have the doctor tend to this," she said.

"Nah. I like our original plan better. Let's just take care of ourselves some more."

"All right. But first let me give you a nice sponge bath."

THIRTY-TWO

The sun rose to shine down upon Byrne with an especially intense heat. Waves poured down from the sky and reflected up from the ground, blurring people's vision as they tried to move where they needed to go and duck back into the heat as quickly as they could.

The wind had died down until it was hardly even a presence, making the summer air all the more stifling. When Clint walked from Shannon's house to Jen's place, he felt as if he'd taken a wrong turn and stumbled into the oven that had cooked the large breakfast that was still fresh in his stomach.

Shannon had gotten up before him and was already at her friend's side. With everything that had happened, she wanted to get to Jen and tell her about the gunfight first, before she heard it from everyone else in town. Clint only hoped that the widow wasn't petrified even more, and he prepared himself for the worst before knocking on Jen's front door.

The only reason he'd allowed Shannon to go to Jen's home first while he ate breakfast was that he figured the next set of gunmen would be watching him. After all, even the most reckless of killers would take a bit of time to recoup after a fight like the one that had happened the previous night.

Besides, Clint had eaten in a little shack of a place run by an old woman living near the railroad tracks. Sitting near a grimy window at one of the place's four tables—something that definitely went against the grain for him—Clint could keep an eye on whoever was coming and going from the residential area where Jen lived. The only ones he saw were a few children going to school and a young woman heading toward the general store with a basket in her hands.

As his knuckles rapped against Jen's door, Clint wondered if he would get any more answers as to what was going on. As much as he hated to think along those lines, he figured he might have to push Jen a little harder to make some progress in that direction.

The door opened and Jen peeked out at him. When she saw who it was, the widow opened the door all the way and said, "Clint, come on in. I was waiting for you."

Clint stepped inside and saw that Shannon was standing in the doorway to the room that they'd been searching the previous night. She gave him a smile and stepped into the short hall.

"Did Shannon tell you about what happened?" Clint asked.

For a moment, Jen got a distant look in her eyes and stared blankly at him. Suddenly, she nodded and crossed her arms in front of herself. "Yes. Yes, she told me."

Getting a bit confused with the way she was acting, Clint looked at Shannon and then back at Jen. "I thought you might have heard the shots. It wasn't too far away."

"Shots? No . . . I didn't hear any shots."

Before Clint could ask another question, Shannon came forward and stood next to Jen. "Could you make us some coffee?"

Hearing that, the widow nodded and smiled warmly.

"Of course I can. Does that sound good, Clint?"

"Uhh . . . yeah. Sure. Coffee would be fine." Waiting until Jen was in the kitchen, Clint turned to Shannon and spoke in a muted voice. "What is going on with—"

"I found this at Jen's bedside," Shannon interrupted. Keeping her body positioned between Clint and the kitchen, she held a small bottle in front of her so only he could see it.

Clint took the bottle and noticed it was still mostly full with a dark brown liquid. After removing the stopper, he lifted the bottle to his nose and took a quick whiff. The smell was unmistakable. "Laudanum?"

Shannon nodded. "I never saw it before, but she has been acting strangely lately."

After pushing the stopper back into the bottle, Clint handed it back to Shannon. "Take this and hide it somewhere. The last thing Jen needs is to be drinking that poison. Where did she even get this stuff?"

"I don't know. Probably from some of Bobby's things. He traveled a lot more and talked about all the things he liked to do when in the bigger towns. This was one of them."

Jen popped her head into view and spoke in a groggy voice that drifted down the hall. "Coffee should be ready in a bit. Anyone want anything else?"

"No, thanks," Clint said. "I already ate." When he saw that Jen had gone back into the kitchen, he turned to look directly at Shannon. "I was hoping to get a little more information out of her today, but I doubt that'll happen anytime soon and I can't wait until she sobers up."

"Don't hold this against her, Clint. She's still a good person."

"I know, but she's still not a help to me at the moment. Do you think you can stay with her until that stuff wears off?"

"Of course."

"When it does, I want you to get her to tell you anything that might shed some light on what's been going on. I need to know exactly why this man wants her dead and why he would kill Bobby. I want details and all of them. Ask if she can help you go through his things. Look for anything that might be the cause of all this.

"If Bobby found something out, I want you to look for what it is and where it is. It's got to be written somewhere, otherwise this whole thing would have ended when he was killed."

"I'll see what I can do."

"Shannon . . . if there's anything else you have to tell me . . . this is the time to do it."

She thought for a second or two and shook her head. "I can't think of anything, Clint, I swear."

Studying her closely, Clint used every instinct and skill he'd learned over his years of reading between people's lines. He didn't see a bit of deception in her face, although he knew better than to take that as gospel. On the other hand, Clint didn't see any reason for her to lie. "All right, then. Get what you can and see what you can find. I'll try to do some digging of my own. Tell me where to find Mr. Prowler."

Reluctantly, Shannon told him about the office of the *Byrne City Examiner*. "Please . . . promise me you'll be careful."

He leaned down and kissed her gently. "I promise." Something else was gnawing at the back of his mind. Before he left, Clint asked Shannon to do one more thing for him.

THIRTY-THREE

Clint only had to wait a minute or two for Shannon to perform the one task he needed. All the while, Jen never came out of the kitchen. Part of him wanted to go in and check on her, but the other part didn't want to see her in the state she was in. Since he hadn't heard any alarming sounds coming from the other room, Clint decided to listen to that second part for the time being.

He only saw her once before he left, shuffling from one part of the kitchen to another as though she was in a world of her own. For her sake, Clint hoped that she would be able to adjust to her own world once the opium wore off.

Before he left, Clint took Shannon aside one more time. "Is there someplace you two can go for a while? Someplace safe that Prowler might not think to look for you?"

"My parents live a few miles out on a farm. I don't think Prowler knows about that."

"Perfect. Go there as soon as you're done talking with . . . no . . . actually, I want you to take her there before you talk to her. Leave here in ten minutes or so. I'll try to give Prowler something else to worry about than what you two are up to."

"Coffee's ready," came Jen's voice from the kitchen.

"Tell her whatever you have to," Clint said as he headed out the door. "Just get yourselves to that farm and make sure nobody follows you. Can you get word back to me if you find out anything else?"

"Ummm . . . yes. I could have my little brother ride back into town."

"Have him leave a message for me at the hotel near the Sundowner. I'll check in there every so often. Now, where's this farm?"

Shannon told him quickly how to get to her family's spread as Jen came walking down the hall toward them.

"Coffee's ready," the widow said.

"I'll pass for now, Jen," Clint explained. "I've got to go. Take care of yourself and go with Shannon, all right?"

Confused, Jen nodded and smiled weakly. "All right."

After giving Shannon a single nod, he squeezed her hands and went out the front door. Before it even closed all the way, Clint could hear Shannon telling Jennifer that they had to get ready to leave right away. He knew there was no time to waste and headed briskly toward Easton Street.

He walked around what seemed to be the back end of the entire town. All he could see besides the hind ends of all of Byrne's main buildings and businesses was a schoolhouse, some garden areas and a pair of churches, one Catholic and the other Presbyterian.

When he turned left onto Easton, Clint walked past the children and a few older women heading toward the school without so much as acknowledging their greetings. His intention was to put them far behind him in case someone else spotted him when he'd turned the corner.

No shots were fired, however, and there wasn't any fuss as he stepped onto the boardwalk and kept going past a carpenter's shop and an undertaker's parlor. The *Byrne City Examiner* office was next in line and Clint walked right up to the matching behemoths guarding the place.

"I want to speak to Prowler," Clint said. *"Now."*

THIRTY-FOUR

Owen Prowler kept him waiting for less than two minutes. That was all the time required for one of the guards to go inside the building, climb the stairs, mention Clint's name and go back down again. When the guard stepped out of the front door, he found Clint waiting right where he'd left him, glaring at the guard who'd stayed at his post.

"Go on in," the first guard said. "All the way back and up the stairs."

Clint didn't want to start any trouble, but that didn't mean he wasn't ready for it. As he stepped through the door, Clint kept his hands at his side and as casual as possible. The muscles inside his arm were tensed, however, and he remained less than half a second away from drawing the pistol.

That need never arose, however. At least, not when he passed the guards and made his way into the office of the *Byrne City Examiner*. Inside, the bottom floor of the office was filled with a large printing press and shelves of metallic letters smudged with ink. The oily smell of ink and grease filled the room, and ink stained the boards beneath his feet. A few men dressed with thick aprons covering plain dark pants and shirts with the sleeves rolled up bustled about the press, talking to one another and making a point to ignore the fact that Clint was even there.

Walking toward the stairs at the back of the room, Clint passed the men and their press and kept walking toward several stacks of paper in the far corner. He started up the stairs, keeping every one of his senses on the alert in case he might be headed into another ambush.

The second floor couldn't have been more different than the first. There, the floors and walls were spotless. The acrid stench of cigar smoke overpowered the odor of ink, and the only sound that could be heard was the muffled remnants of the voices downstairs and the tapping of boots against the floor.

Standing in the short hall with a single door on either side, Clint saw a shape fill up the doorway to his left and he instinctively stepped away from the stairs. His hand remained at his side, but he was ready to draw at the first sign of provocation.

The shape in the doorway came out into the hallway, revealing itself as the lean, polished figure of Owen Prowler. His gray eyes narrowed slightly as he peered out at his guest. "Mr. Adams?"

"That's right," Clint said. "Would you be Owen Prowler?"

"I certainly would. Please . . . come into my office and have a seat."

Clint walked toward the doorway, waiting for Prowler to step back into the office before quickly moving past the top of the stairs. When he got inside the sparsely furnished room, he noticed that Prowler was watching him like the proverbial hawk.

Hooking his thumb back toward the stairs, Clint said, "I'm still a little hesitant to turn my back on your men. After what happened last night, I'm sure you understand."

Prowler moved around his desk and stood between it and his own chair. "Last night? Ah, yes. You must be referring to that young apprentice of mine who was gunned down at the train depot."

"Yes. I was also referring to those three you sent after me and Miss Carsey in the street later on."

Cringing as though genuinely hurt by the words, Prowler nodded solemnly. "That was quite the mess. All the same, though, I'm willing to let bygones be bygones. Have a seat."

Clint waited for the other man to lower himself into his chair before reaching behind him and pulling the office door shut. "If you don't mind."

"Of course." Easing his shoulders back, Prowler allowed the gun in his shoulder holster to fall forward just enough for it to be seen. "I don't mind in the slightest."

Walking around the chair, Clint went over to the front of the desk and leaned forward with his hands resting on top of the polished wood. "If you think I didn't see that fancy gun of yours the moment I laid eyes on you, then you must think I'm either blind or stupid. Either way . . . you're gravely mistaken."

Prowler said nothing. Instead, he reached for the cigar box and started to open it. Before his fingernail could even get beneath the lid, he felt a hand close around it and stop it from moving another inch. His eyes hadn't caught so much as a hint of movement from Clint.

"Like I said, Prowler . . . still a little fidgety."

Both men stared at each other for a moment before Clint released Prowler's wrist and opened the cigar box for himself. All he could see was a row of precisely rolled smokes lined up from one end of the box to another.

"Care for one, Mr. Adams?"

Clint dug his hand into the cigars, past the first two rows and to the bottom. From there, he removed his hand—as well as the derringer that had been hidden beneath all the fine tobacco.

Grinning, Clint said, "Don't mind if I do."

THIRTY-FIVE

"You're an intelligent man, Mr. Adams," Prowler said as he helped himself to a cigar and sat down in his chair. "Then, I guess you would have to be to survive for so long with a reputation such as yours."

Clint took the derringer he'd discovered and walked over to one of the shelves that was farthest away from Prowler's desk. Setting the two-shot weapon onto the top shelf, he said, "And I guessed you wouldn't show me that gun in your shoulder holster unless you already had another in reserve."

With a flick of his wrist, Prowler scratched a match across the top of his desk and lit his cigar. "Touché."

"I didn't come here to trade quips with you. And I didn't come in here to start any trouble."

"Not yet anyway," Prowler said under his breath.

"That's right. Not yet."

"Then why did you come here? Was it to come to the aid of that poor little widow that you seem to have taken a liking to for no apparent reason?"

Clint locked eyes with the other man and nodded once. "Actually, yes. And I'd appreciate knowing just why you feel the need to go after an ailing woman when you already gunned down her husband."

Prowler's laugh was so sudden that it sent a puff of smoke from his nostrils. "I thought you were a well-traveled man, Adams. That drunk woman's only ailment is her addiction to that vile substance that would have sent her husband to an early grave if I hadn't beaten him to it."

"Then you admit to killing him?"

"I never denied it."

"Why?" Clint asked. "What's this all about?"

"And why should I tell you?"

"Because I'm asking nicely. And if you keep going back and forth with me about this, I might not ask so nicely the next time." Reaching out with one hand, Clint took one of the several similarly bound volumes from the shelf closest to him. "And if things turn ugly, your little business in this town might just go up in smoke quicker than that log you're sucking on right now."

Prowler's face turned to cold, rigid stone. His eyes fixed on the book in Clint's hand and his upper lip slowly curled back from his teeth. "Put that back."

"What's the matter?" Clint asked with a wry grin. "You have any prewritten confessions in here?"

"You wouldn't be able to understand what's in there, so just put it back."

Clint flipped open the book, mostly as a way to get under Prowler's skin. He didn't like the way the other man was circling around everything that had been said, and he figured that he might slip up if he got flustered. When he opened the cover and started flipping through the pages, however, Clint felt a little pang of frustration in himself.

Either Prowler was a good enough judge of character to read that on Clint's face, or he was used to such reactions from others who'd tried to read his journals. "You see? I told you that you wouldn't be able to understand what's in those."

Scanning through the entries, Clint saw that the writing was arranged in paragraphs and sentences, complete with punctuation, but the words themselves simply appeared to be gibberish. They didn't even bear resemblance to any kind language he'd ever laid eyes on.

"What is this?" Clint asked. "Some kind of code?"

"Those are my personal memoirs and yes . . . they're in a code of my own devising."

Slamming the book shut, Clint kept hold of the journal for the simple reason that it seemed to bother Prowler. "You barter in information, right?"

Prowler shrugged. "Anyone in town could tell you that much."

"And Robert Dawson got ahold of some of that information, didn't he?"

"Let the dead rest in peace, Adams. It's no use to try and—"

"He got some of your precious information, didn't he?" Clint interrupted. He put enough emphasis on his words to snap Prowler out of his self-satisfied smugness.

Nodding once, Prowler said, "That's right. He poked his nose where it didn't belong and it got him killed. I'm sure he's not the only man who's stopped breathing for that reason. I know for damn sure that he won't be the last."

When he said that final sentence, Prowler glared at Clint with enough venom in his eyes to drop a buffalo. Clint returned the glare in kind. He wasn't the type to openly intimidate people, but he wasn't a stranger to the process either.

Both men fought their silent battle of wills for only a few seconds, but those seconds dragged by on feet of lead. In the end, it was Prowler who looked away first; a sizeable victory in a battle of that nature.

"I don't take kindly to men like you, Prowler. You prey on anyone at all by scraping up whatever dirt you can on as many people as you can. You think you sit higher than everyone else, but even the lowest hired gun makes his living by doing his own dirty work. You have to hide behind coded ledgers and guards posted outside your door.

"You think you can get over on me by sending your stooges to ambush me in the night when I'm trying to help a woman get around in her own town. You know who I am, so you must also know that I don't scare too easily. But I'm a fair man, and since I know that Bobby did his share of shady dealing, I'm willing to let the matter drop as long as you leave his widow and Shannon Carsey alone."

"Is that all?" Prowler asked sarcastically.

"There's one other thing. I want to know exactly why you're after her."

"She has something that belongs to me." Leaning forward like a hawk preparing to swoop down on its prey, Prowler said, "She knows what it is. They *both* do. Once I have it back, we can all go back to our normal lives. Until then . . . those two, as well as whoever is foolish enough to associate with them, don't have much of a life to look forward to."

Clint could tell he wasn't about to get much further with him just then. The main reason he'd gone there at all was to get a feel for the man face-to-face. That was the only way for him to truly know what he was dealing with, and now that he'd actually met the man that was threatening the two women under his protection, Clint figured that he'd accomplished more than enough to justify his visit.

The other reason he'd gone was to draw all of Prowler's many eyes onto him while Shannon and Jen got out of Byrne. Clint went to the door and pulled it open. He immediately saw three armed men standing there, poised and ready to leap into the office. Glancing past them, Clint could see several other shapes at the bottom of the stairs, which were most definitely not the gangly workers operating the printing press.

Unless Prowler had half the town acting as his own personal guards, Clint figured that most of them had to be present and accounted for. He didn't rule out the possibility that one or two might still be following Shannon, but even he couldn't be everywhere at once.

Sometimes, no matter how high the stakes, a man had to gamble.

"I assume I've made my point," Prowler said in a smug tone.

Clint locked eyes with one of the guards and twitched as though he might go for his gun. The guard snapped back and fumbled for his own weapon. Before he got close to clearing leather, Clint was already smiling back at Prowler. "And I know I've made mine. Good day to you . . . I'll just show myself out."

THIRTY-SIX

Clint took his time making his way down the stairs and walking through the first floor of the *Examiner*. He made a point to observe every one of the armed men, sizing each one up in his own mind as to how much of a threat he thought the man might be. Although he knew better than to trust such initial observations completely, Clint was also still buying as much time as possible to cover Shannon and Jen's escape.

Every moment that Clint kept those guards watching him, he knew that those men couldn't be going after the women. Beyond that, Clint also figured that if someone was watching the women, they wouldn't leave town after them without checking in with their boss first.

Clint emerged from the *Examiner* building and checked the watch in his pocket. It was a new, copper-colored piece that he'd bought in New York City, and it still shone when the light came anywhere near it. All in all, he'd killed twenty minutes since he'd left Jen's house. He could probably count on the men watching him for at least another five, which should be plenty of time for Shannon to get Jen onto a wagon and head out of town.

At least, Clint hoped it would be enough time.

144

Strolling as though he didn't have a care in the world, Clint walked a little ways down the boardwalk, retracing the path he'd taken to get to the office. All the while, he was counting off the moments in his head while listening to the sound of heavy footsteps on the boardwalk behind him.

He didn't have to look over his shoulder to know that Prowler was watching him from his office window as well. Clint could feel the other man's eyes boring through the back of his head like a bone saw chiseling away at his skull.

Clint's arms hung casually at his sides, but the muscles were tensed and every one of his senses was waiting for the first sign of an attack. The footsteps had stopped and the low rumble of voices drifted through the air. Looking over at a local who was passing by, Clint tipped his hat and studied that person's face.

It was a woman in her fifties clutching her handbag as if she thought Clint might try and take it from her. She looked scared, but not as panicked as she would be if there were several guns pointed at Clint's back.

"Good day, ma'am," Clint said.

She didn't return the greeting and picked up her pace.

Clint kept walking and didn't relax until he knew he'd gone out of the range of the pistols he'd seen around the guards' waists. After a few more steps, he turned and looked around him as he kept moving forward, scanning the rooftops for any signs of movement. If there were riflemen up there, they were keeping their heads down for the time being, which was just fine with Clint.

He made his way across the street and into an open area on the outskirts of the little town. Clustered there were a few cabins, a large home, and the Catholic church he'd seen on his way from Jen's place. Clint walked straight past the homes and quickly stepped into the shadow of the cross that was cast down upon the ground from the church.

The church was larger than the Presbyterian house of worship nearby and looked as though it could accommodate most of the townsfolk if they all decided to gather there. At the moment, the doors were propped open and there were only a few people drifting in and out.

Clint stepped into the church and noticed that four of the five locals in there headed for the door the moment they saw who it was that had come inside. With all that had happened since his arrival, Clint didn't blame those folks in the least for wanting to distance themselves from him. In fact, he stepped aside so as not to stand in their way.

"Welcome, my son," said a lean man dressed in black pants and jacket. He wore a priest's collar around his neck and approached Clint with a wide, comforting smile.

"Hello, Father. I'm—"

"Clint Adams, I know." In response to Clint's somewhat surprised look, the priest said, "Even for one who gets out as little as I do, word travels fast in a town this size. I'm Father Connell."

Clint shook the hand that the father offered and couldn't help but feel at ease around the man. Father Connell was roughly Clint's height, with a full, cheerful face and a strong grip. His skin was darkly tanned and he moved with an anxious fluidity.

"Some of my parishioners have come to me with some concerns of late."

"Concerning me?" Clint asked.

Father Connell blushed slightly and grinned apologetically. "I hate to say it, but . . . yes. There has been a sense of unease that has many people in town talking about a great many things. Unfortunately, much of that talk is probably exaggerated."

Clint started walking toward the ornately carved altar

at the front of the church. The priest fell into step beside him as they walked down the center aisle, past several solidly built, if somewhat chipped, wooden pews. The walls were decorated with paintings depicting several peaceful scenes, ranging across the entire spectrum of heaven and hell.

"I hate to say it, but plenty of what you hear might not be as much of an exaggeration as you may think."

Nodding slowly, the priest clasped his hands in front of him. A look was growing on his face that reminded Clint of the way a child looks when they're dying to tell a secret that has been burning a hole in their tongue. "Actually, I've heard some things about you that didn't exactly come from my parishioners. Wait here just a second."

And before Clint could stop him, the priest hurried off to a narrow door that almost blended completely into the wall to the left of the altar. Father Connell opened the door, disappeared through it for a few seconds, and then reemerged carrying something in both hands.

"I got this from a salesman who came through town while I was working in Dodge City," Father Connell said while extending both hands. He was holding a paperback novel with a well-worn cover and pages that had yellowed at the edges. It's title was *The Smoking Colt—A Tale of The Gunsmith*.

Clint rolled his eyes and muttered, "Aw, Jesus Chr—"

THIRTY-SEVEN

Clint stopped himself before he risked offending the very house he'd entered. When he looked back up at Father Connell, he cringed slightly and said, "Sorry about that, Father."

The priest looked as though he was just on the verge of getting his nose out of joint, but he pulled back just in time. "Ask for forgiveness, and it shall be given." In a conspiratorial whisper, he added, "Just don't let it happen again."

"How many of those books did that salesman have?"

"Not many," Father Connell said as he looked down at the yellowback novel in his hands. "And only this one about you. I think they sold most of those before I got to them."

Clint was just about to take some comfort from what the priest had said—right up to the point when he heard that there were, indeed, plenty more of those things out there.

As much as seeing his life distorted and bandied about for everyone to see riled him, Clint put that aside for the moment and pulled his mind back to the business at hand.

"Actually, I came to see you about something besides that, Father."

The priest put the novel down and looked seriously at Clint. "I thought so. You wanted to confide in me about those men you killed?"

Even though the statement had come from a priest, Clint was still taken a little by surprise. "Well . . . uhh . . . no. That's not why I came here, either."

Now it was Father Connell's turn to look surprised. "After killing those men the other day, you don't feel the need for forgiveness?"

"My life was in danger, Father. And I was trying to protect two people whose lives were in danger also."

"True enough and those are extreme circumstances."

Thinking that he was in the clear for the moment on that issue, Clint was about to start talking again when he saw that Father Connell had closed his eyes and was speaking silently while forming a cross in the air before him. Once Clint heard that the priest was reciting a prayer, he lowered his head and waited for Father Connell to finish.

"There," the priest said, lifting his head and looking much more refreshed than he had only a few seconds ago. "Now what is it that you wanted to speak to me about?"

Clint reached into his pocket and removed the item that he'd asked Shannon to get for him before he'd left Jen's house. The mourner's Bible fit in the palm of his hand, and when he held it out, Clint said, "This is why I wanted to talk to you. I hope you can help me."

Father Connell looked down at what Clint was holding and nodded. "May I?" he asked, reaching out toward the little book.

Clint nodded and allowed the priest to take the book that he'd been holding. Father Connell flipped through the first couple pages and turned to a passage that was written by hand at the top of one of the initial sections.

"I gave this book to Jennifer Dawson on the day of her husband's funeral. I wrote this passage myself, since the edition left by her dearly departed Robert wasn't the same one that I favor."

Clint stopped short for a moment. "Bobby left this book for her?"

"Yes. I suspect that he knew his life was in danger a short while before he was killed. He came to me himself and made a few simple requests. Giving his wife this particular book was one of those requests."

"I thought the funeral home gave those out. Or maybe the church?"

"I usually provide a mourner's Bible to help any family members in need of comfort. At those difficult times, I like to go over the scriptures with those left behind. It's such a conflicted time. There are so many questions and so few answers."

Sensing that he was on the verge of opening a theological can of worms, Clint tried to steer the priest back on track. "But Bobby had this book and specifically gave it to you for Jen if anything was to happen to him?"

"Yes. That's pretty much the way it was."

"Is there anything unusual about him making such a request?"

Father Connell furrowed his brow and thought about it for a few seconds before nodding. "It is unusual, but at times like those when a man is facing such mortal danger . . . peculiar things might go through his mind. He had a friend who worked at the *Examiner*'s printing press and I believe it was his way of getting his affairs in order."

"Then Bobby knew that his life was in danger?"

"Oh yes." The priest's face darkened a bit when he said that. "Many people in town knew it, although we didn't know why."

After the encounters he'd had with Prowler, Clint figured that Bobby must have been through every one of that man's scare tactics before the lead started to fly. His getting shot was a foregone conclusion. There was something else in what the priest had said that perked Clint's interest.

"Now, you mentioned something about this 'edition' of the mourner's Bible. Are there a lot of different ones?"

Taking another couple seconds to think, Father Connell shrugged and said, "I would think so. I've seen one or two in my time, but they're usually pretty much the same. There are a few subtle differences in the approach they take to apply the teachings of the scripture to—"

"I hate to interrupt you, Father, but I am in a bit of a hurry."

"Oh, of course. I'm sorry." Perusing the mourner's Bible, Father Connell shook his head as he got to some of the later passages. "I've seen a few different editions, but not one with quite so much . . . I guess you'd call it . . . extraneous material."

Clint reached over and turned to one of the sections in the back that were bent at the top. "I wanted to ask you about . . . this here," he said, pointing to a page covered with words he hadn't been able to read. "Do you know what that is?"

Father Connell took a moment and read through squinted eyes. "Well . . . these lines here are Latin."

"What do they say?"

"I could translate it for you, but it appears to be samples of Gospel that are printed in English in the front of the book. It might be easier for me to mark which ones they are because they seem to be verbatim."

"I'd appreciate that," Clint said. "Now, you said 'those lines' were Latin. They're not all Latin?"

"No. Definitely not. These lines beneath this set here and . . . well . . . actually it looks as though every other line is written in . . ." The priest shook his head and shrugged. "I hate to say it, but I don't really know what language that is for sure."

"Any guesses?"

Once again, the priest looked down at the little book and studied it. He read the pages with such intense concentration that Clint could see the strain showing at the corner of the other man's eyes. "I studied several languages at the seminary, but this doesn't look like any of them. In fact . . . it really doesn't look like any language at all."

"What's that supposed to mean?"

"It means the letters aren't even arranged in what looks like words. Here," Father Connell said while turning the book so Clint could see it right-side-up. "Take a look for yourself."

When Clint looked at the writings this time, he only focused on every other line, instead of the entire thing as a whole. Unlike the first time he'd laid eyes on the mourner's Bible, it didn't look completely alien to him. "I'll be . . ."

"You have any ideas?" the priest asked as a gentle way to cut him off before any more colorful language emerged from Clint's mouth.

"Actually . . . I *have* seen that other writing before!"

THIRTY-EIGHT

Clint knew that Prowler's men would be waiting for him to come out of that church. If the situation had been different, he might have looked for another way out of the building rather than stroll right back out where the armed men could see him. But since he was actually hoping to keep those men watching him for as long as possible, Clint did exactly that.

Leaving the priest in a mild state of confusion, Clint took the mourner's Bible back, thanked Father Connell for his time and then strolled right back out where the armed men could see him.

"Mr. Adams," Father Connell called to his back. "If you're in danger as well, I might be able to help you in some way."

Clint was in the front doorway, looking out at the guards who were scattered along the street, waiting for him. "That's all right, Father. You've helped me more than you know."

"Then can you do something for me?"

Turning to look over his shoulder, Clint saw the priest stoop down, pick something up and come walking toward him. "What can I do for you?" he asked once the holy man was approaching.

Father Connell held out his hands and extended the yellowback novel toward Clint. "Could you sign this?"

"Would it be all right if that waited for a better time?"

"Oh . . . of course," the priest said sheepishly as he noticed the guards standing outside glaring at Clint. "Some other time." Before he went back inside the church, Father Connell gave each of the gunmen he could find a stern, disapproving glare.

If the priest's silent scolding had any effect, it must have been strictly on the gunmen's souls, because not a single one of Prowler's men so much as flinched in response. Father Connell seemed happy with his effort all the same and patted Clint on the shoulder before taking his reading back to his chambers.

Clint shut the door to the church and walked down the steps leading to the street. The closest gunman to him was standing beside the large home next to the church. Some others were in the street and on the boardwalk on either side. Ignoring every last one of them, Clint walked down Easton until he could step onto the boardwalk across from the *Examiner* office.

He could only hope that all those guards had been gathering and milling about outside while he'd been in the church. That would mean that Shannon had had that much more time to get Jen to her family's farm. Before Clint had walked to the next storefront, he was already thinking about what his next set of moves would be.

If he had been the only one involved in the situation, a more direct approach could be used. But Clint wasn't the only one sitting across from Prowler as if they were staring each other down over a chessboard. There were other innocent people involved.

Well . . . the more he thought about it . . . Clint was

starting to wonder just how innocent one of them truly was.

But before he could get any firm answers on that matter, he had to go on the assumption that both Jen and Shannon were still in need of his protection. He'd done what he could by sending them off, but he doubted that would buy him much more than the rest of the day. After listening to the priest talk, he knew that news traveled awfully fast around the town of Byrne. It seemed to travel even faster than Clint would normally expect for such a small town.

Clint kept walking past the saddle and harness store and straight up to the narrow building that served as Sheriff Larkins's office. The door was propped open by a stool, so Clint walked straight inside and up to a desk, which was one of the few pieces of furnishing in the room.

Sheriff Larkins sat leaning back in his chair with both his feet resting on top of his desk. When he saw Clint walk in, the lawman nodded and touched the tip of his hat by way of a greeting.

"Nice day, isn't it, Adams?"

"I'll save that judgment for later. How are your prisoners doing?"

"Look for yerself," the sheriff said as he hooked his thumb back to the narrow cage sectioning off the rear quarter of the room.

Sure enough, when Clint looked back there, he saw both of the farmhands laying in the cell. One of them was on the cot with his gunshot wound wrapped in layers of bandages. The other sat with his back against the wall and his head slumped down to his chest.

"Glad you came to see me," Larkins said. "I been meaning to talk to you about that ruckus that was kicked up on Track Walk last night."

"Well, before you get ahead of yourself, you should know that I didn't start that ruckus."

Larkins held up both hands and held his palms out in a soothing manner. "Don't get all riled up. I heard more accounts than I could handle regarding the matter and nearly every one of 'em says that you were defending yourself as well as Miss Carsey."

"*Nearly* every one of them?"

The lawman shrugged. "Every one that I can believe, anyway."

"Then what do you want to talk to me about?"

"I was just going to ask how much longer you were planning on staying in Byrne."

Clint shook his head. "You sound eager to be rid of me, Sheriff."

"Well, no offense, but this town was nice and quiet until your train pulled into it. Ever since then, I've had my hands full with more shootings than I ever had in the span of my career."

"What about the shooting that took Robert Dawson's life? Did you hassle the man who did that like you're hassling me right now?"

Swinging his feet down off his desk, Larkins got up from his chair and squared his shoulders with Clint. "Bob Dawson was a friend of mine and he was killed outside of my jurisdiction."

"And I'll bet that made you feel real bad, didn't it, Sheriff? I'll just bet that you had one hell of a speech lined up for whoever pulled that trigger."

For the next couple of seconds, both men stared at each other with fires burning deep in their eyes. The older man with the badge pinned to his chest dug his fingers through the shaggy gray hair that hung down from beneath his hat. The thick bristles covering his upper lip trembled slightly as he exhaled several strong breaths.

Just the fact that Larkins hadn't done much besides take statements and arrange for the bodies to be moved told Clint what kind of a lawman he was. Unfortunately, if

Larkins had been truthful in saying that he was good friends with Bobby Dawson, that might not look too good for him either. The only lawmen that Bobby ever liked were the kind that could be bought for a price a working man could afford.

But if Larkins was crooked, he wasn't bent beyond all repair. Clint knew that the moment he'd gone in and seen both farmhands still warming the floor inside the jail cell. Apparently, Sheriff Larkins was just overly lazy. At least that cut down the number of guns on the streets of Byrne by two.

Larkins seethed. "Are you gonna answer my question or not?"

"I'm not planning on staking any claims here in town, if that's what you're asking. And as soon as my business is finished, I'll be more than happy to let you get back to your nap."

"That's just fine. Now, what other business do you have with me?"

Taking one last look at the pair in the cell, Clint nodded. "I've seen what I came for."

With that, Clint turned on his heel and walked out.

THIRTY-NINE

"What the hell is he doing now?"

Owen Prowler asked the question in a low grumble while staring out of his office window. His hands were clasped behind his back and his back was ramrod straight.

Although there was a guard in the room with him, the gunman knew better than to try and answer the question. He'd made that mistake once before when the hawklike man had been speaking to himself, and nearly got his head bit off for his trouble. So this time, the guard kept still and didn't move from his post in the doorway at the top of the stairs.

Prowler stood just outside the pool of light that spilled in through the glass. It was too bright outside for him to remain in total shadow, but enough of him was concealed to keep him from being easily spotted from the street. From his perch, he'd been able to watch Clint walk to the church and then down the street to the sheriff's office. Now, he could see as Clint once again stepped outside.

He followed the figure in the street with his eyes as his mind turned over and over again inside his head. Turning his head slightly, Prowler looked toward the guard behind him without taking his eyes away from the window.

"Go down and ask if anyone knows what he's been doing."

The guard nodded and walked down the stairs.

Prowler heard the footsteps recede and kept watching the street until Clint disappeared from view. At that moment, the footsteps were already coming back up the stairs.

"I thought I told you to check with the others," he said while turning on the balls of his feet to set his eyes on the guard as he walked into his office. But the man who came up the stairs wasn't the same one he'd sent away. In fact, it was the man he'd sent away several hours ago.

The tall, muscular guard stepped into Prowler's office, filling up most of the doorway with his bulk. He was the same man who'd followed Clint and Shannon the night before.

"Ahhh," Prowler said. "I was wondering when you'd have something to report. Come in."

The guard entered the office and stood next to the other chair, but did not sit down. "Both of the women are gone," he said.

"Gone? Where would they go?"

"They loaded up Miss Dawson's wagon and headed out less than an hour ago. I followed them as they pulled out of town and kept behind them for almost a mile."

Prowler's eyes slowly shut and his jaw set into a firm line. "Please don't tell me you simply let them get away from you so you could come back here."

Despite his much larger size, the guard seemed almost cowed by Prowler's tone. "I let them go, but only when I figured out where they were going."

"And where might that be?"

"They turned off of the main road pretty quick. And since they only took a couple bags that they could carry, it's a safe bet that they weren't going that far. The only place in that direction that's less than a couple days' ride is a farmer's spread that Miss Carsey went to a month or two ago."

"She went there before?" Prowler asked, raising his eyebrow.

"Yes, sir. I followed her there once when this whole thing was just about to start up. You'd put me on the job of checking up on all of Bob Dawson's acquaintances."

Prowler nodded slowly. The tension that had been pouring from him eased off a bit as well. "So you think they're going to that farm? Is it possible she might have seen you following her and was trying to draw you in the wrong direction to shake you?"

"No, sir." When he said those two words, the guard couldn't have packed them with any more certainty. Judging by the look in his eyes, he was as sure about that answer as he was about his own name.

"All right then. Take a few of the others with you and go out to that farm. I want you to drag those two bitches back to town even if you have to pull them by their hair."

"How many should I take with me?"

"As many as you need. I'll trust your judgment."

"And what if someone at that farm tries to get in our way?"

Remaining silent for a moment or two, Prowler let that question roll around in his mind before opening his mouth to answer. Finally, in a low, raspy voice, he said, "If anyone gets in your way . . . I want you to hurt them. I've left the heavy-handed tactics behind for too long, and too many people are starting to get the idea they can walk all over me."

The guard nodded again and let the orders sink in. His posture became just a little more rigid, and his face appeared to shift into stone as he steeled himself to the notion of violence. "How bad do you want them hurt, Mr. Prowler?"

"If they get in your way . . . hurt them bad. If they insist on making nuisances of themselves, put them down for good."

"Yes, sir."

With that, the guard turned around and headed out the door. Before he could get to the stairs, he was stopped by Prowler's sharp, piercing bark of a voice.

"The ones you don't take with you . . . send them after Clint Adams. But wait until you and your team are well on their way."

"You don't want to leave any here with you?"

Prowler shook his head. "That won't be necessary. Adams won't come back here right away. When he does, I can face him alone. If that second group is doing their job, they should be right on his tail anyway."

The guard paused at the top of the stairs, looking into the office with uncertainty in his eyes. "Are you sure that's wise?"

Prowler's single nod, coupled with the fire that blazed in his stare, was enough to move the guard down the stairs and on his way. When the bigger man was gone, Prowler turned back to the shelf where Clint had been standing. His hand flashed to his shoulder holster and drew the silver-plated .38 in the blink of an eye.

"Come at me, Adams," he said under his breath. "And I'll bury you right next to your friend."

FORTY

As soon as Clint turned the corner onto Ridgemont Avenue, he picked up his pace and hurried all the way down the street until he was at the train tracks. From there, he turned left and headed straight for the livery stable next to the train depot.

He didn't have to look behind him to know that he would be followed. Clint could feel the eyes on his back like hornets' wings brushing against his shoulder blades. Even so, he figured Prowler's men would be cocky enough being on their own territory that they wouldn't have to keep him in their sights at all times.

Knowing well enough that he couldn't rely on much of anything since just about anyone could be informing to Prowler, Clint got to the livery and went to Eclipse's stall.

"Howdy, there," the liveryman said. "You come for that Darley Arabian?"

"I sure did. Help me get him saddled up and ready to go."

Reacting to Clint's fast pace, the liveryman jumped to his feet and met Clint at the stall. He was already tossing a thin blanket over the stallion's back as Clint was hefting his saddle with both hands. Between the two of them, they got Eclipse ready to ride in record time. When he was done, the liveryman stood back, looked at Clint proudly and held out his hand palm up.

"That was a hell of a race," the liveryman said. "Glad I was up to the challenge, if you know what I mean."

"Yeah, I know what you mean," Clint answered while digging into his pocket. He removed two dollars and gave one to the other man. "That's for the race. And this," he added, holding the second dollar, "is for doing your best to forget about where I went after riding out of here."

The liveryman nodded and winked. "I gotcha. Some folks in town might pay a lot for that sort of information, huh?"

"Yes, they would. And if I can tell anyone following me got turned in the wrong direction, I'll be back to pay more for the effort."

"Understood."

Clint wasn't sure if the liveryman would help him or not, but he wasn't about to waste any more time with him, either. He did get a good feeling about the other man when he saw that the guy had already run to the back of the stable and opened a door leading straight out onto the open prairie.

As soon as Clint had ridden out of the stables, he touched his heels to Eclipse's sides and hung on. The stallion was more than happy for the excuse to pour out some of the steam that had been building up over the last several days. Being cooped up in train cars and livery stalls, the Darley Arabian had been aching for the chance to cut loose.

With a jolt of motion, Eclipse thundered through the tall, swaying grass and flew away from Byrne. Clint let the stallion run full out for a bit and then steered him in the right direction, toward the farm that Shannon had told him about.

After a minute or so, he looked over his shoulder and

studied the movements in his wake. As far as he could tell, the only things stirring there were grass and dust. He couldn't spot any pursuers just yet, but that didn't mean his path would be clear.

When dealing with a man who dealt in information as much as Prowler, Clint always figured that someone somewhere knew what he was doing. That way, Clint was always prepared for it.

Someone could have followed Jen's wagon. Someone could have ambushed them along the way. Someone might be coming after them later. Clint kept all of those possibilities open in the back of his mind. It was too late to second-guess his decisions now. All he could do was make the best ones he could and then run with them.

For the moment, Clint let his mind relax.

He'd chosen his plan of attack and was carrying it out. All he could do just then was hold on and let Eclipse do his running for him.

The Darley Arabian thundered beneath him, his black mane rippling in the wind as he tore over the prairie. His hooves pounded against the dirt with so much power that Clint thought he could feel the earth rocking beneath them.

At times like those, Clint felt completely at ease. No matter what else was going on or how many other wheels were turning around him, once Eclipse was running at a full clip, all Clint needed to do was hang on.

The only bad thing about Eclipse running at full speed was that the trips never lasted too long. In a shorter amount of time than Clint would have thought possible, he could make out the shape of a modest farmhouse sitting next to a barn that was a perfect match for the one Shannon had described.

FORTY-ONE

When Clint rode close enough to the farmhouse, he could see several figures coming forward to meet him. He couldn't tell if they were smiling or frowning, but he could most definitely tell they were all carrying guns. By the looks of them, the rifles and shotguns were mostly the kind that would be used for hunting, which gave Clint some hope that they were being wielded by the farmers themselves.

One figure came forward faster than the others, and it wasn't long before Clint could hear Shannon's voice calling out over the thunder of Eclipse's hooves. She waved her hands over her head and kept on running right past the line of men who fanned out and lifted their guns to their shoulders.

Clint slowed Eclipse down and pulled him to a stop outside the range of most of those guns. Shannon kept running toward him and was nearly out of breath by the time she got to Clint's side.

"Thank God," she said as he dropped down from the saddle. "I was hoping Prowler wouldn't try something else before you could get away."

Before Clint could respond, he was wrapping his arms

165

around Shannon and trying to keep from being knocked over by her enthusiastic embrace. She kissed him on the lips and held him as tight as her arms would allow. Finally, she broke away from him and pressed her face against his shoulder.

"I knew you'd make it," she said thankfully. "I knew it."

Nodding toward the line of men slowly approaching him, Clint asked, "What about them?"

Shannon looked at the other men as though she'd forgotten completely about them. "Oh, those are my cousins and uncles. I told them I recognized your horse, but they wanted to be sure."

"Maybe you should have a talk with them pretty quickly. They don't seem to be lowering their guns."

Spinning around, she waved toward them and shouted, "It's all right. I told you I recognized him."

"You sure?" one of the men shouted.

Rolling her eyes, she said, "Yes I'm sure! Put those guns down."

There was a bit of hushed conversation among the men as they kept walking forward. By the time they got close enough for Clint to see their faces, they had lowered their weapons. One of the older men left the rest of them behind and came up to stand directly in front of Clint.

That man held out his hand and stared Clint directly in the eyes. "You best be takin' good care of this here girl."

Trying to keep his expression as honorable as possible, Clint nodded and shook the man's hand. He got the impression that the other man was the strict, old-fashioned type, and he spoke to him as such. "Of course, sir. I came out here to protect her. Actually, I want to try and protect you all."

Although the man's eyes were stern and piercing, he grinned ever so slightly and hefted the rifle in his other hand. "We can take care of our own jus' fine."

Clint's first impression of their weaponry had been correct. Most of them were old hunting rifles, a few of which were still loaded musket-style. The rest were shotguns and an old Henry that seemed to be several models behind the ones currently on the market.

Even so, Shannon's relatives made up for quality with quantity, since there were still more of them pouring out of the barn and farmhouse. The ones making up the first wave had gathered around Clint and Shannon, staring at him as if they thought he might sprout horns and start running on all fours.

"We should all get inside," Clint said. "I don't think I was followed, but I wouldn't count on us being out here alone for very long."

"Sure 'nuff," the older man said and led the others back toward the weathered buildings.

Shannon and Clint followed the others, keeping back far enough so they could talk without being heard by the entire clan.

"I've got good news and bad news," Clint said.

Shannon held onto his hand, squeezing it as she asked, "What's the bad news?"

"Prowler isn't going to wait too much longer before making another move on us. In fact, I wouldn't be surprised if he tried to end this whole thing in the next day or two. Maybe even sooner."

"How do you know that?"

"Because I met with him. I got a chance to look into his eyes, and I take him as the sort who doesn't like loose ends hanging around. He's the type who survives by being the one making all the first moves, and he doesn't like someone else pressing his hand. Therefore, he'll either have to hold back or run forward even faster."

Smiling weakly, Shannon glanced over at him. "Maybe he'll hold back."

Clint shook his head, thinking back to the way he'd

spoken to Prowler and the way Prowler had looked at him when they were both in his office. "No. He'll run. I made sure of that."

Clint could feel the nervousness that flowed off of Shannon like an invisible wave. Her grip tightened around his hand and she became suddenly quiet.

"But that's not necessarily a bad thing," Clint quickly said. "He's going to make his move, and I'd rather have it come sooner than later." Clint stopped when he was about ten feet away from the front door of the farmhouse. He held Shannon by the shoulders and looked squarely into her eyes once he knew he had her complete attention.

"This has been a whole lot of unpleasant business," he said. "But it's going to be over soon. There's still a bit of storm to get through, but I'll help you and Jen get through it. Prowler is wound up tight right now, which means he'll be snapping at us real soon.

"When a man snaps, he moves too fast, and that's when he makes a mistake. When he makes a mistake, that makes it all the easier to beat him at his own game."

She brightened up a little, but still seemed to have some doubt. "I tried talking to Jen. She either wouldn't tell me anything or she didn't know anything to tell. After all this is done and the shooting's over, I'm worried that Mr. Prowler will just get his business back in order."

"Actually," Clint said. "That brings me to my good news."

FORTY-TWO

As Clint and Shannon went inside the farmhouse, some of her armed relatives surrounded the place with their guns tucked under their arms. Looking out at them, Clint felt like he was in some kind of military camp with sentries patrolling the grounds and himself inside discussing strategy. After refusing a couple offers from some of Shannon's aunts for food or water, Clint led her to a room where they could sit down and talk without interruption.

They were in a sitting room in the middle of the house. Each of them sat perched on the end of a rocker with a low table in between their chairs. Clint took out the mourner's Bible from Jen's house and set it on the table. He asked for some paper and a pencil and didn't have to wait too long before one of Shannon's aunts came back with the supplies.

Flipping through the book, Clint told Shannon a quick version of his discussion with Father Connell as well as his conversation with Prowler in the *Examiner* office. With that done, he opened the Bible to one of the pages covered with unreadable text.

"This," he said, pointing to one line in the Bible, "is Latin. Father Connell confirmed that. But this," he said, pointing to the line below the first one, "isn't anything either of us could make sense of. Now, Father Connell said this Latin writing is a straight translation for . . . this passage," he said while flipping to the page that the priest had shown him.

Shannon was looking confused. "I don't see how any of this helps, Clint. Why would Prowler care about this Bible?"

"He wouldn't care about a mourner's Bible. That's why Bobby put this information in it. Otherwise, it never would have gotten into Jen's hands at all."

Nodding, Shannon let Clint speak, even though she clearly didn't know where he was headed.

Clint picked up the pencil he was given and quickly copied the English version of the text that was printed in Latin in the Bible. Once that was done, he flipped back to the page with the Latin text and copied down the lines of gibberish below the lines of English he'd just written.

Now more lost than ever, Shannon started to fidget in her chair. When she was just about to say something, she saw Clint lift a finger and then hold his hand up as if to ask for just a couple more seconds of indulgence. She decided to give him that much and waited until he was done copying the lines.

"OK," Clint said once he was done. "Now, either this will work out just right, or I've completely wasted a bunch of time that we don't have."

"If that's supposed to make me feel better, you failed miserably," Shannon said. But since Clint seemed to be fully absorbed in what he was doing, she sat back, tried to calm herself, and let him do it.

Clint had started writing on another part of the paper. Switching his eyes between the English and gibberish words, he compiled a list that ran down the entire side of his paper. The list itself wasn't too complicated. It was simply a series of two-letter combinations, the letters separated by dashes. He went slowly at first, but by the time he was past the fifteenth of these, his writing became faster and faster.

Finally, once the list was twenty-six pairs long, Clint sat back and looked at Shannon. "A waste of time . . . or the biggest piece of this entire puzzle? Now's the time where we find that out."

"Clint, I still don't know what you're—"

"Please, Shannon. I'm almost there. Just work with me on this last little test."

"Fine," she said over a heavy sigh. "What do you want me to do?"

Clint picked up the Bible, found one of the Latin/gibberish passages, and then marked the English version of that same Latin text with a scrap of paper torn off the sheet he was using. "All right," he said while handing the open Bible to Shannon. "Every other line, starting with the top one, is Latin. I want you to read me the letters of every other line starting with the *second* line."

"You mean the ones that don't make any sense?"

"Exactly."

Shannon read off the gibberish lines letter by letter until she reached the end of the paragraph. All the while, Clint compared those letters to the list he'd created and then worked on piecing together another paragraph on his sheet of paper.

The entire process took a couple minutes, and when they were done, Shannon set the Bible down on her lap and looked at him as though she'd lost the last scrap of her patience.

Clint looked over the paragraph he'd pieced together, smiled and said, "For we who live are always delivered to death for Jesus' sake, that the life of Jesus also may be manifested in our mortal flesh."

When he saw Shannon looking at him with confusion, Clint held up that passage written in his hand.

"Did you get that from the letters I read?" she asked. Clint nodded.

"The nonsense letters?"

He nodded again.

"How?"

Taking the Bible from her hand, Clint held it open and looked at it. "That isn't nonsense. It's code. The Latin is there to hide it, but it's also a way to help us translate it. Once I got a way to translate the Latin into something I could understand, I pictured the nonsense letters beneath the English translation and made my list. The list is the key, telling me how the nonsense matches up to our alphabet."

"How did you know it would match the English?"

"Because I figured whoever put it there was probably not fluent in Latin. Besides, I know I made the right key because it allowed me to translate this passage from those lines of nonsense you rattled off to me."

"I'm impressed, Clint. But I still don't see what—"

As she spoke, both of them could hear Shannon's relatives shouting at each other and the house. A couple shots were fired, which set the entire family on alert. Shannon jumped to her feet and looked as though she wanted to jump all the way out of her skin.

"I still don't see what this has to do with Mr. Prowler," she said quickly.

Clint was still calm as he rose to his feet and held the mourner's Bible out in front of him. "That nonsense is like a made-up language. I may not have been able to read Latin, but I recognized it enough to have an idea that that was what those other lines were. And once I'd seen that code, I kept it in mind. But more than that . . . I recognized it when I saw it in Mr. Prowler's office."

No more shots besides the warning shots were being fired. Still, men were rushing by the windows and storming into the house, shouting instructions to the women and children inside. Shannon kept her eyes on Clint as some of his anxiousness began to flood into her. For the first time during his demonstration, she was beginning to feel as though she knew *exactly* where he was headed.

"You saw that in Prowler's office?" she asked.

"That's right. He had a journal full of it and there were shelves full of those journals. Didn't you tell me that Prowler made his living by keeping hold of other people's dirty secrets?"

"I sure did."

"And he's got to keep those secrets somewhere."

Smiling, Shannon stepped forward and looked down at the mourner's Bible for herself. "I'll be damned. Bobby not only found out where Prowler's secrets are, but he cracked the code as well."

"And then he made sure to pass the key on to Jen. That's one hell of an inheritance."

FORTY-THREE

With the mourner's Bible tucked safely in his pocket, Clint made sure Shannon was tucked away just as safely before he headed outside. He was immediately met by the older man who'd greeted him when he'd first arrived. By the looks of him, he was the general of this little army of Carseys.

"They're comin', Mr. Adams," the old man said.

Clint fell into step beside the old-timer and followed him away from the farmhouse. "How many?" he asked.

"My youngest is scoutin' from a tree over yonder. He sent word that he saw at least four of 'em ridin' like their tails was on fire."

Clint looked to where the old man was pointing and saw a kid no more than eight years old sitting on the ground. His face was red and he was sucking in breath after making the run from the edge of their property.

"They can't be more'n a quarter mile out by now," the old man explained. "That is, if they're ridin' as fast as you were."

Clint figured the riders were probably closer than that, but he didn't want to contradict the old man in front of all his boys. The important thing was that all of them

174

seemed ready to protect their home. After taking a quick count of the cousins and uncles, who were all armed with rifles or shotguns, Clint looked to the old man and asked, "Are there always this many of you here?"

"Nah. When we heard about what happened to poor ol' Bobby, some of these here boys came all the way in from Coyville to lend a hand."

"And has there been any trouble here since then?"

"Nope," the old man said, shaking his head. "We ain't even had to go off this farm too much. Are you fixin' to help us take the fight to these fellas?"

Clint shook his head. "Actually, I don't think I'll have to."

After saying that, Clint pointed out a couple prime spots for the men to form two firing lines. There were rows of crops and enough tall grass for the men to take up their positions and keep from being seen. The entire process took less than a minute or two. In fact, it was harder to keep the men quiet as they waited for the approaching horses to close in.

The gunmen sent by Prowler thundered over the prairie with their eyes trained on the farm ahead. When they could make out the two separate buildings, they drew their weapons and came to a stop.

"That the place?" one of them asked.

The man in charge of the other three nodded. "That's it. Mr. Prowler said the women should be there and that they need to die. If anyone gets in our way . . . send them to hell right alongside the bitches."

All of the gunmen seemed to like the sound of that and nodded their approval. Their fists were clenched around their guns as though they were already savoring the heat they would feel once they started firing. Without another word passing between them, they put the spurs to their horses and bolted toward the farm.

There was a line of trees which they figured marked the edge of the farmer's property. All four horses charged past those trees and kept going.

Next, they came to a field of waving grass which mingled with a crop of poorly tended wheat. The stalks weren't too healthy, and if the gunmen had been so inclined to notice such things, even they would have seen that nobody would be getting rich on that farm anytime soon.

But they weren't there to survey crops, and they kept riding with their eyes focused on the battered old house which drew closer with every passing second. They thundered into the waving grass like soldiers charging into a waist-high stream. Their guns were held high and their eyes were dead set upon their ultimate goal.

If their eyes had been focused on the land directly in front of them, they might have seen the first line of shabbily dressed men as they straightened up and set off a round of gunfire that roared straight into the gunmen's faces.

All of the gunmen on horseback were taken off their guard as their entire field of vision was washed over with gritty, blazing smoke. Chunks of lead whipped through the air as a few more shots were added to the mix. A few of the rounds slapped against flesh, knocking a pair of the riders clean out of their saddles and dropping them onto the ground.

The rifles might not have been the latest models, but they functioned well enough to serve their purpose. When the pair of Prowler's shooters hit the ground, they were sporting huge, gaping wounds that would take their lives in a matter of minutes.

The remaining pair of riders pulled back on their reins and started firing into the line of men. Their aim was still thrown off by the cloud of smoke that had enveloped them, and besides that, their targets had already ducked back down into hiding.

Both killers rode through the smoke and came out within ten yards of the farmhouse's front porch. Their goal was still first on their minds as they set their eyes on their target. With their nerves still jangling from the first onslaught, they were looking for motion around them, and they found it a second later.

The rest of Shannon's extended family leapt out from where they'd been hiding and pulled their triggers. The old man was among that second wave, and his hunting rifle blasted a hole into the lead rider's chest. Of those last ones that fired, only three of the cousins struck what they were shooting at . . . but those hits were more than enough.

The rider toppled from his mount, bleeding from several fresh holes in his stomach and upper chest, and headed toward the ground at an awkward angle. The side of his face hit first, twisting his neck as the rest of his weight fell on top of him, snapping his spine into two separate pieces.

Clint stepped out of the house and holstered his Colt. Looking to the old man, he said, "I think the ladies are in good hands here. I've got some business in town."

FORTY-FOUR

Clint knew he was being followed.

In fact, not only did he know it, but he also took great comfort from the fact that a couple more of Prowler's men were riding behind him as he steered Eclipse back into Byrne. After all the ones that were either hurt or killed over the last couple of days, that left Prowler with very few soldiers under his command.

Clint wouldn't have been surprised in the least if the ones following him were the last of the bunch. One thing he knew was that those killers were sure as hell not going anywhere near the farm outside of town.

Slowing Eclipse to a quick walk, Clint headed straight down Ridgemont Avenue and turned onto Easton. He clearly saw two men coming up fast behind him, but that didn't concern him in the least. Rather than worry about them, he hitched Eclipse to the rail outside of the *Byrne City Examiner* and walked up onto the boardwalk.

"You can't go in there," said the bigger of the two guards as Clint swung down off his horse. His boots touched down in the street directly in front of the newspaper office.

Clint stopped and turned around. "You'd be wise not to try and stop me."

"It's my job to stop you."

"No!" came a voice from above. "It's your job to do as I say!" Looking down from his office window, Owen Prowler fixed his gray eyes on the big tracker. "I told you to follow Adams here. Now let him come up since he seems so inclined to do so. I'll let you know when to take the next step."

Reluctantly, both of the guards relaxed their stances and allowed Clint to enter the building without getting in his way.

Clint was ready to act on a moment's notice as he went into the *Examiner* office and moved past the press and toward the stairs. He stepped lively all the way up to the second floor and didn't hear the front door open until he was nearly at Prowler's office.

The bald, clean-shaven man stood behind his desk with his arms crossed in front of himself. He watched as Clint walked into his office and headed straight for one of the many shelves. "I can be a good man for you to know, Adams," he said smugly, without making a move to stop Clint from taking one of the ledgers and opening it. "We could be a lot of help to one another."

"It's too late for that," Clint said, leafing through the coded pages. As his eyes scanned the gibberish words, he found that the pages were set up with headings and lists scattered throughout the entire volume. All he had to do was figure out the first couple letters of a few of the headings for him to quickly get a handle on what the lists contained.

"Those books won't do you a bit of good," Prowler announced. "But with my help, that can change."

"I don't need your help. I've already cracked your code."

For the first time, Prowler's stony facade broke. He

recovered quickly, however, and shook his head. "You're bluffing."

"Am I?" Turning to the open ledger, Clint recited, "Judges. Here in Kansas from Wichita all the way to the state court. I could read you a couple names, but I don't have to do that for you to know I'm right."

Prowler's facade cracked again. This time, however, it stayed cracked.

Just to push him even further, Clint flipped pages and made some quick translations. "And there's also a few sheriffs in here, huh? Impressive."

"But those are . . . you couldn't . . ."

"It's not that hard of a code, really," Clint told him. "Shifting the alphabet a couple notches one way or another. I memorized the system myself, but the key's all written out for those who need to see it in black and white. It might help to get all this dirty laundry cleaned up for good."

"I can pay you, Adams. Or I could help you find some information that might benefit you." He was sounding desperate now. Even as the two guards came up the stairs, Prowler sounded like every bit of steel within him was buckling inward. "We can work something out. Whatever you want, I can arrange for it."

Without missing a beat, Clint said, "Turn yourself in to the law. Confess to all the killings you've arranged, starting with the death of Robert Dawson, and burn every last one of these ledgers."

By the look on Prowler's face, Clint might just as well have asked him to chew his own arms and legs off. "That's not . . ." Stopping, he straightened up and let a dark resolve fall over his features. "I won't have you blackmail me."

"What's the matter? Don't like being on the receiving end?"

Both guards began to move into the office, but Prowler kept them back with a flick of his hand. "I'll take care of you myself. Just like any good king, I've got to handle some battles myself."

Clint smiled grimly. "Is that how you see yourself? As a king? How sad."

Prowler's eyes glazed over with an almost metallic sheen. The muscles in his jaw tensed and his hand inched toward the silver-plated .38 hanging in his shoulder holster.

It was obvious that any more talk would be wasted, but Clint opted to waste it just the same. "You don't have to do this, Prowler. You can turn yourself in and face a judge. With any luck . . . it won't be one of the ones in that ledger."

All cockiness and arrogance that had been in Prowler's eyes was snuffed out, leaving only fatal resolve to follow through on what he'd started. His mouth was a line etched in stone and his eyes were cold and lifeless.

Clint kept his eyes on Prowler and his ears straining for any sound of motion from the guards. Before the strain of splitting his attention could weigh down on him, he saw a flicker of movement as Prowler went for his gun.

The man was fast as he plucked the .38 from its holster. Prowler cleared leather and got his finger beneath the trigger guard by the time Clint had drawn his modified Colt and took his shot.

Not many others had gotten that far before Clint Adams took them down. Of course . . . they were all just as dead.

The Colt barked once and drilled a hole through Prowler's skull. Before the .38 could drop from the twitching corpse's hand, Clint had spun around to aim the pistol at both guards. "You get the same chance. Take it and live . . . or gamble your lives for a dead man."

Both of the guards hadn't even gotten the chance to

draw. After watching their employer fall face-first onto his desk, they both unbuckled their gun belts and let them fall to the floor.

"All right," Clint said. "One of you fetch me a match."

Watch for

The Rat's Nest

258th novel in the exciting GUNSMITH series
from Jove

Coming in June!

Explore the exciting Old West with one of the men who made it wild!

AVAILABLE WHEREVER BOOKS ARE SOLD OR TO ORDER CALL:

1-800-788-6262

(Ad # B112)